"Jess, calm down. I won't hurt you."

The words made no sense to her muddled brain, but they continued, quiet and assured. "It's all right. I won't let anything happen to you."

It wasn't the words that made her sink into him, but the voice that, even after all this time, she'd recognize anywhere. Her eyes hadn't been playing tricks on her that afternoon. Will Gumble was in this compound. In her very room.

How could he act so casual? As if it hadn't been ten years since they'd spoken? As if he hadn't just shown up in a foreign country where she was being held prisoner? As if the very sight of him didn't make her knees weak with relief?

"I thought I saw you— I thought that was you, but..." Her stomach pitched, fear and relief mingling with alarm and the echo of a remembered betrayal. "What are you doing here?"

His lopsided grin hadn't changed. "Your dad sent me."

"My dad?" Forcing a chuckle, she said, "I figured when my dad realized I was missing, he'd send a SEAL team to bring me home."

"Not a full team—he just sent one."

Books by Liz Johnson

Love Inspired Suspense

The Kidnapping of Kenzie Thorn
Vanishing Act
Code of Justice
*A Promise to Protect
*SEAL Under Siege
Stolen Memories
*Navy SEAL Noel

*Men of Valor

LIZ JOHNSON

graduated from Northern Arizona University in Flagstaff with a degree in public relations and now works as a nonfiction marketing manager for a Christian publisher. She finds time to write late at night and is a two-time ACFW Carol Award finalist. Liz makes her home in Nashville, TN, where she enjoys theater, exploring the local music scene and making frequent trips to Arizona to dote on her nieces and nephews. She loves stories of true love with happy endings and blogs about her adventures in writing at www.lizjohnsonbooks.com.

Navy SEAL Noel

Liz Johnson

HARLEQUIN® LOVE INSPIRED® SUSPENSE

Recycling programs
for this product may
not exist in your area.

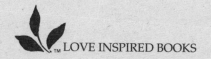 ™ LOVE INSPIRED BOOKS

ISBN-13: 978-0-373-67650-7

Navy SEAL Noel

www.Harlequin.com

Printed in U.S.A.

No one will be able to stand against you all the days of your life. As I was with Moses, so I will be with you; I will never leave you nor forsake you.
—*Joshua* 1:5

A friend loves at all times,
and a brother is born for a time of adversity.
—*Proverbs* 17:17

For Katie Bond
who daily demonstrates the meaning
of true friendship.
I am so thankful for you.

And for Jess Barnes
who always makes me laugh and lent me her name
for a character.
I'm stunned by your talent and grace.

ONE

Petty Officer Will Gumble could have gone his whole life without seeing Captain Sean McCoy again.

In fact, he'd been counting on it.

But he wasn't about to risk ignoring a summons from the brand-new executive officer of the Naval Amphibious Base Coronado. Even if it was worded as a request and asked for a meeting at The Cue, a pool bar well off the base and away from the regular SEAL watering holes.

Will tugged on the sleeves of his civilian jacket and took a deep breath before jerking the door open. Noise and the vapour of electronic cigarettes surrounded him as he stepped inside, scanning the hazy room for threats, exits and friends. In that order.

Two guys next to the pool table by the wall pushed each other, knocking a row of empty glasses onto the green felt. They'd had too much to drink, but weren't worth a second look. A girl who didn't look old enough to even be in the bar leaned against the jukebox and flirted with the gray-haired man beside her. She looked up and caught Will's eye. Hers brightened, a slow smile forming on too-red lips.

Will looked away fast.

The last thing he needed was a girl latching onto him in front of his new XO.

He slipped between two tables, pushing toward the back of the room, finishing his survey. The place wasn't particularly crowded, given the weekday night, but the green and blue neon lights made faces almost unrecognizable.

What if he couldn't identify the captain? He hadn't seen him in more than ten years, and McCoy had been none too happy on that occasion. In fact, the last time they'd met, McCoy had been downright red in the face to see his little girl sneaking into the house at zero dark hundred. Will hadn't exactly meant to drop Jess off so late, but he'd been a reckless kid, cocky and assured. And when the old navy man had clamped a hand on his shoulder and stared hard at him, Will had nearly buckled. Would he be able to recognize McCoy without the searing anger and disapproval in the older man's expression—or would both still be there, even after all these years?

When he reached the last booth in the farthest corner, all concern about recognizing Jess's dad vanished in an instant. Captain McCoy hadn't aged much. Still broad, with an angular jaw, and barely a wrinkle around his narrow eyes. He kept his black hair in a traditional military cut, and in the light any hint of gray was indistinguishable. But there *was* something different about him. McCoy, who had always stood so proudly, slumped in the vinyl booth, head bowed over a half-empty glass. He seemed intent on examining the surface of the table, but his mind was clearly engaged elsewhere.

Will walked over and waited for the other man to acknowledge him. When McCoy glanced up, his eyes turned into slits, a frown firmly in place. "I don't need anything."

Maybe Will was the one who had changed.

Ten years, thirty pounds and a SEAL Trident pin would do that to a man.

Or maybe it was just the haze hanging over the room.

"Captain McCoy?" Will kept his words short, in case he reverted back to that eighteen-year-old kid whose voice had had a habit of cracking under pressure.

McCoy squinted harder before jumping out of the booth to assess him more closely. After a long pause, he said, "William?"

"Yes, sir." He held out his hand, expecting

a shake, but McCoy clapped him on the back, nearly hugging him.

"It's good to see you, son. I almost didn't recognize you out of uniform." Not the reaction Will had been expecting, but it was a far cry better than the alternative. McCoy motioned to the table and slid back into the booth. Will sat down opposite him. "How are your parents? Still living in the area?"

"They're fine, sir. Dad just retired, and they moved closer to the beach so he can surf more."

The captain chuckled silently, his shoulders bobbing and a few wrinkles forming on either side of his mouth. But the humor never reached his eyes, which were pained. He wrapped his hands around his glass of soda and gazed into the dark brown liquid.

Will opened his mouth to ask about Jess, but snapped it closed before the words could pop out. He had no right to ask how she was doing or what she'd done in the past decade. Not even if she'd ever gotten married, settled down, had a family.

The pain wasn't as acute as it had been at first, but the idea of his childhood best friend married to someone else still hit him like a punch in the stomach. At least he knew she hadn't married his brother, Salvador. That's why they'd stopped talking—because Jess had said she was thinking about accepting Sal's promise ring. And because

Will had decided that ignoring her phone calls was the best way to deal with the pain those words had caused.

Well, that and because he'd done the only thing he could think of to get away from having to watch Jess marry his older brother. He'd joined the navy, shipped out for parts unknown and made no effort to keep in touch. He only knew that she hadn't married Sal—hadn't even accepted his ring and had broken Sal's heart in the process. His mom had told him that much.

Will didn't have any right to ask how Jess was doing, so he canned the small talk and asked the important question.

"You wanted to meet me, sir. What can I do for you?"

McCoy released a breath that deflated his shoulders, the dim light in his eyes vanishing altogether. He glanced toward the front door before clearing his throat. "I need your help."

"Yes, sir." Will bit his tongue to keep from asking why the captain hadn't asked for this meeting to take place in his office on Coronado.

Turning his glass in endless circles, the older man stared hard at the bouncing ice cubes. The seconds ticked by as the ambient noise built around them, a group singing their hearts out by the jukebox leading the charge.

"I need this conversation to stay off the record."

Will leaned forward, his elbows spread and arms resting on the sticky tabletop. "All right."

"You're under no obligation to agree to what I'm about to ask you to do." Will nodded, but McCoy continued as though he hadn't noticed. "If this goes badly, it could cost me my commission and you your place on the teams."

Will swallowed a lump that had lodged somewhere below his Adam's apple. This was his chance to walk away. McCoy was giving him an out before he knew too much. If he stuck around, he'd be privy to information that was bound to get them both in trouble.

But he hadn't been summoned by chance. None of the other men on his boat crew had been invited. McCoy had called him specifically.

If the tingling of his spine was any indication, it had everything to do with their past acquaintance.

"Something happened to Jess." It wasn't a question, and as the words tumbled out of Will's mouth, his stomach rolled. His Jess. His best friend from junior high to graduation. If she needed him, she was in trouble, and the situation was worse than he could imagine. Batting down the accompanying nausea, he squinted across the table. "Tell me everything."

Jabbing his fingers through his hair, McCoy let out a slow breath. "Jessalynn is working on her PhD in bioengineering and had a grant to study an airborne pathogen at Southern California State University."

Will let out a low whistle, the sound involuntary and ill equipped to convey how impressive he found her achievements.

"Three days ago she was working late in the lab. The security alarm went off about oh one hundred, and when the guard arrived, the lab had been ransacked. Jess and her bioweapon had vanished."

Fire shot through Will's forehead and he covered his face with his hands, praying this was some sort of sick joke. But the XO sat in equally stunned silence, as if this was the first time he'd spoken the truth aloud.

Massaging his temples, Will growled low in the back of his throat. "Who took her?"

"The DEA thinks that it's a Panamanian drug cartel."

"And they want what?"

McCoy's face crumpled in silent agony. Just seeing it made Will's chest hurt, and he clawed at his T-shirt, searching for air, the smell of alcohol and perfume catching in his throat. He could picture Jess's bright grin and the mischievous twinkle in her eyes. But he could not picture her in Panama, fear etching her facial features until they were unrecognizable.

This was a hoax. Someone was playing a cruel joke.

His Jess couldn't be at the hands of some drug cartel. She was safe and sound. And probably long-ago married to someone who actually deserved her.

Except the tortured voice of a father unable to save his only child wasn't easily conjured. It carried with it the pain of broken hearts and lost dreams.

Sean McCoy wasn't tricking him. He was a man in need of help.

Will closed his eyes, pursed his lips until they almost touched the tip of his nose and released a pent-up breath. "Let me guess. They want to use the pathogen and need someone to release it for them."

"A friend at the DEA says there's a bitter land war going on down there between two cartels. Bringing in a biological weapon seems very in character. Unfortunately, since they're only attacking each other rather than targeting civilians, the DEA isn't interested in getting involved, as long as it's not crossing over our borders."

"Doesn't kidnapping an American count as crossing our borders?"

He shook his head. "They can't definitively prove who was behind the abduction. And they're about as eager to poke around drug cartels as a mouse would be to wake a snoring bobcat."

"What about the government? Why don't they send a team down to extract her?"

McCoy closed his eyes. "There's not enough intel to know exactly where she's been taken. They're searching all of Panama right now, but the jungle is dense, and it could be weeks before they have enough info to send in an extraction team."

The captain's unspoken words hung between them. Jess didn't have weeks to spare.

With folded hands pressed to his wrinkled forehead, Will pinched his eyes closed. Someone had to go after Jess. She wouldn't survive for long after the cartel got what they wanted. Once she'd served her purpose, they would have no need for her.

His middle clenched, as if he was preparing for a blow from an opponent in the boxing ring. The truth hit harder than any fist.

The cartel would dispose of her. Soon.

He'd always thought he'd have a chance to end their decade of silence. And a bunch of drug-slinging bioterrorists weren't going to take that chance from him. He owed her an apology, and he would make sure he had a chance to deliver it.

Pressing flat hands to the tabletop, he gazed

into McCoy's haunted eyes across the table. "What is it you want me to do?"

Another sigh. Another droop to the wide shoulders. "The United States Navy has no official jurisdiction in this situation. Officially, they have no information about it and absolutely no plans for a rescue attempt."

"I understand."

"Do you?" Bushy eyebrows pulled together, and a flicker of something akin to hope appeared in the captain's hazel eyes, so much like his daughter's.

"Yes, sir. I'm going to need approval for a short leave of absence."

For the first time that evening, the corner of McCoy's mouth quirked upward in a true smile. "Done."

"I'll be out of touch. Completely." He stared hard at the older man, wishing he could come right out and tell the tough truth. But now that Will had agreed, McCoy needed to set up some plausible deniability. The captain couldn't know the details. If a superior officer started asking questions, he'd have to tell the truth. No details meant no lies.

The XO hadn't asked Will to do anything. No orders. Not even a suggestion. Just a conversation in a seedy bar far from the base and further from their norm. No one would recognize them enough to pinpoint that this was the night their lives changed.

But they were about to.

"I understand," McCoy said.

Eager tension built in his legs, and Will nodded toward the door. "I'd better get going." He slid across the bench and zipped his jacket as he rose.

The captain followed his movements, trailing him between the pool tables and into the starlit parking lot. Gusts of fresh air were like a lifeboat to a man who didn't know he was drowning. The sweet scent of the breeze wrapped around him, and he took deep breaths through his nose until his mind was clear of everything but the mission ahead of him.

"Thank you." The older man's voice was lower, more gravelly.

Will nodded, but didn't directly respond. Instead he said, "Please let her husband know that I'll do everything I can."

McCoy shoved his hands into the pockets of his blue jeans and cocked his head to the side, his ear almost to his shoulder. "Her husband?"

His palms suddenly sweaty, Will rubbed them against his pants. Was McCoy just pulling his leg or was it possible that she'd never settled down? Jess marrying someone—anyone—else had been the reason for ten years of silence. Was it possible she'd never gotten married at all?

The questions running through his mind must have been broadcast on his face because the captain let out a low chuckle. "Oh, Jess quit dating about the time you disappeared."

Will nodded, confusion mixing with an unnamed emotion in his chest and leaving him speechless.

"She said she'd rather focus on her education. I tried to talk to her about it, but she didn't have much to say on the matter. I wish like fire that her mother had been around for that. She'd have known what to say. Instead I bumbled through, and Jessalynn told me not to worry about it, so I let it go."

The words tumbled around Will's mind as he tried to make sense of them. Finally, they reemerged as a question as smooth as sandpaper. "Then Jess is—she's not—she's never gotten married?"

"No. She's not married." The captain offered a fraction of a grin. Maybe it was just a twitch, but it sure looked like more. Like an invitation to be a man instead of running like the boy he'd been all those years before.

McCoy clapped him on the back before striding toward his car. Halfway there, he spun around with a loose shrug of one shoulder. "Try not to start a war, son."

"Yes, sir. I'll try."

But no promises. If it took a war to save Jess, he'd start and end it.

When three sharp cracks broke the air on the opposite side of the lush courtyard, Jessalynn McCoy fell to the lawn, dropping the box she'd been carrying and covering her head with both hands.

"Up! Up!" The man with the large black gun slung across his chest, dressed head to toe in green camouflage, dug the tip of his boot into her ribs. She cringed, curling into the pain, her already labored breaths coming out in quick puffs. He hadn't fired the warning shots, but she didn't doubt that he was willing to shoot at anything. Even her.

Pushing shaking hands beneath her, she glared up into the shadowed face of her guard, Manuel. He was charged with keeping her inside the compound and lugging a myriad of outdated scientific equipment to the room they'd deemed a laboratory. He frowned and spit toward her, barely missing her shoulder. She glared at him, jerking away from the spot next to her hand where the disgusting stream had landed.

Manuel grunted, kicked her foot and pointed his gun at the broken beakers and hot plates scattered at her side. They didn't need to speak the same language for her to understand what he wanted. When she didn't move immediately, he wrapped his hand around her arm. Jess jerked it away, her skin crawling under the touch of his callused fingers.

Why couldn't they just leave her alone?

Every morning they insisted on marching her from her cell of a room to the kitchen for a spicy breakfast and then pushing her from the storage shed to the lab and back, carrying supplies that had probably been upgraded about the time Louis Pasteur started studying biology.

She didn't bother voicing her complaints. What good would it do? She wasn't a guest. She was a prisoner. And so she kept her mouth shut and her eyes on the exits, dreaming up wildly improbable escape plans.

Realistically, she knew she'd never be able to get away on her own. She didn't even know what country she was in. Even if she could scale an outside security wall and scramble over the loops of barbed wire and shards of glass without getting snagged, she had no idea what she'd face on the other side, or how she would get to help.

She was stuck inside this steaming, muddy compound—with or without a personal escort.

At least until she could figure out a plausible plan.

Or until her dad sent help.

Manuel shoved her shoulder, and she whispered, "God, please let him send help soon."

"Qué?" Manuel shook his dark hair off his forehead, his eyes boring into her.

Jess swallowed and blinked, fighting the urge to look away. "Nothing." She didn't wait for him to push her again, but stooped to collect the scattered debris.

The weight of the full box in her arms made each step through the dewy grass twice as hard, three times as slow. She was losing strength, her energy reserves depleting quickly from too much manual labor and too many nights with not enough sleep.

She wasn't about to risk more than just the essential catnaps at night.

Someone had been poking around outside her room the night before.

She wasn't going to be asleep if they managed to make it in.

Exhaustion was wearing her down, but she didn't have a choice about setting up her lab, as ordered. Manuel seemed far too eager to use his gun, taking every opportunity to butt the barrel against her. Like a teenager given his first car, Manuel couldn't wait to take it for a test drive.

When they reached one of the nondescript gray, cinder block buildings that seemed to multiply within the compound, Manuel went to work on the large, padlocked metal door. It squealed as he pushed it open and motioned for her to follow him in.

Jess stumbled over the four-inch step, her legs like overcooked fettuccine. With a clinking of glass, the box she'd been carrying landed on one of four black tables evenly spaced in the middle of the room. The table's wooden legs slid on the cement floor as Jess fell against it.

Manuel grumbled and motioned for her to rearrange the furniture.

If they'd spoken the same language, she'd have told him that this high school chemistry class replica—complete with two full walls of counter space and one measly window—was more likely to cause them all to be killed than keep the Morsyni toxin safe until it was released.

At least, she assumed that's what they wanted her to do. Really, it was all a guess at this point. Manuel's monosyllabic grunts and broken English had barely hinted at why she'd been attacked, drugged and dragged to…wherever this was. But it wasn't a far jump to guess that it had everything to do with her research on the Morsyni toxin. Before three men in black ski masks had abducted her from the Southern California State University lab, they'd forced her to retrieve her sample vial of the powder. She had just one gram of the ultrafine substance, but it contained more than a trillion lethal spores.

Which was enough to kill fifty million people. Or more.

Jess's stomach lurched at the very thought. Her research had all been targeted at better understanding the Morsyni, hoping to one day find a cure. Or at least a way to minimize its effects. But whoever had brought her here just wanted to twist her expertise and use it against... Well, she didn't know who. But someone was a target, and she had been set up to be the arrow.

Suddenly the humidity wasn't the only thing making it hard to breathe. She pushed past Manuel and out the door, hoping that the narrow alley along the back of the cinder block barrack would provide enough air to lift the band around her chest.

They could have only one reason for taking her, too. They needed someone who knew how to release the toxin without killing everyone inside the compound.

Manuel shoved her shoulder, gesturing her back to the storage shed to get more supplies. "Move." He locked the door and then resumed breathing on her neck. She shuddered at the stale odor, praying once again to be anywhere but confined by these compound walls with this man as her tail.

She'd nearly worn the winding path to the shed into a muddy trench, but she kept her head down as she trudged toward their destination.

They emerged into the courtyard, the afternoon sun steaming her skin through her cotton shirt. They had to be near the equator. Or possibly on the sun.

Jess was nearly all the way across the courtyard when her foot disappeared into a mud puddle, and she lurched to the ground, landing on all fours.

Manuel yelled at her, and she glared over her shoulder at him.

"Ocho días." He rolled his eyes in a universal sign of displeasure. *"Sólo ocho días."*

Eight days. Only eight days.

Even she, who'd passed high school Spanish only because of her best friend, could translate that. Manuel expected to have to put up with her for only eight more days. It was too much to hope that he'd simply be replaced by a different guard at the end of that time or that she'd be free to leave then.

Which could only mean one thing.

She'd have served her purpose. In eight days, she'd be expected to release the toxin.

And then she'd likely be killed.

Unless she escaped.

Something like fear and dread clawed at her insides, leaving a twisted trail of pain in its wake.

She fought the sudden need to vomit, and gulped in great quantities of oxygen.

"Up!"

Pushing her hands into the mud, Jess made it to her feet, and her gaze fell squarely on a man in a tattered gray suit twenty yards away. Two armed guards held his elbows as he glowered at another one, who seemed to be in charge. The man in the gray suit turned a blank stare on her, his pale face cloaked in a five-o'clock shadow. And devoid of any recognition.

But she knew him.

She'd known him more than half her life, though she hadn't seen him in years.

At least…at least it looked like Will.

Her heart leaped to her throat, lodging there as she tried to call out.

Manuel stepped into her line of sight, and by the time she'd scrambled to look around him, the familiar face had disappeared.

Maybe the heat and humidity were causing hallucinations. Maybe she'd simply imagined him, hoping someone would come for her.

But why would her mind conjure Will Gumble?

"Vámanos." Manuel nudged her toward the giant house that took up nearly half of a security wall. Its golden stucco walls and clay-tile roof were out of place among the host of intentionally unremarkable buildings in its shadow. It had to

be home to the man or men in charge, although she'd yet to see them.

She followed the path around the big house to the storage shed, pushing all thoughts of Will Gumble out of her mind. She had eight days— less, actually—to make it out of this place alive. And dwelling on her former best friend wasn't going to rescue her. She had to find a way out on her own.

TWO

Jess huddled in the farthest corner of her cell, behind the bed where she'd managed to filch only a few hours of sleep the past few nights. The lumpy mattress and loose bedsprings stood like a sentinel between her and the doorway now, but they wouldn't be much protection if anyone came in.

She grasped the foot-long wrench she'd stolen off a maintenance cart three days before, holding it vertical and ready to swing if her worst nightmare crashed through that door. Her eyes had adjusted to the darkness of the windowless room enough that she could make out the rotting slats of the lower part of the door by the crack of light seeping beneath it.

Despite plenty of threatening noises every night since her arrival, no one had unlocked the bolt on the outside of the door. Not yet. But if someone did, she'd be ready for him.

She crouched for what felt like hours, unable to tell the exact passage of time, but the transition from screaming pain to a dull ache to numbness in her thighs was better than a clock.

In the loose haze between alertness and the siren call of sleep, her mind began to wander to the familiar face she'd seen that afternoon. Of course, it couldn't possibly have been Will. She hadn't seen him in ten years. She probably wouldn't recognize him even if they sat face-to-face. The man had just resembled him. Dark brown hair and a jaw chiseled into a blunt point. From that distance, she'd only gotten the impression of dark eyes that probably bore no resemblance to the milk-chocolate ones she remembered. And the man who'd entered the compound today had worn a very dark, very handsome five-o'clock shadow. Will had never been able to grow much facial hair.

Well, eighteen-year-old Will hadn't, anyway.

A gentle thud against the door sent her heart into overdrive, all traces of sleep tossed aside. She leaned forward, her grip on the wrench sending spasms through her fingers. Taking a shaky breath, she blinked into the darkness as the telltale rattle of a doorknob sounded. The inside lock held. But for how long?

A shadow briefly blocked the light seeping beneath the door, the feet there moving soundlessly.

She gasped for breath, the heavy, humid air like a wet towel draped across her nose and mouth.

It was now or never. She could wait for the man to enter, to investigate the room and find her in the corner. Or she could face him with the element of surprise.

She scrambled toward the entrance, the sound of her shuffling feet echoing against the cinder blocks no matter how she tried to muffle her steps.

A hiccup surprised her, and she slapped her palm over her mouth to mute the obnoxious noise.

The lock clicked, and she held her breath as she slipped behind the door, painfully swallowing another hiccup. The sound of her pounding heart seemed to fill the room as the flimsy wooden slats swung open, leaving a narrow beam from the courtyard security light spilling across the floor. The shadow of a broad man filled the gap. His movements silent, his motions sure, he closed the door after stepping inside.

This was her only chance. Her only hope of protecting herself.

If Jess could fight him off now, maybe word would spread that she wasn't to be trifled with.

The wrench weighed more than a school bus, and was almost as unwieldy, as she swung it toward his head. She had to knock him out, or at least to the ground. Then maybe she could even make a run for it.

Just before the metal connected with the barely

visible outline of his skull, he ducked and lifted an arm. The tool glanced off his shoulder, grazing his neck. In a flash he grabbed it, and before she could let go, he jerked it behind her back, leaving her arm twisted and useless. Fire screamed up to her kinked shoulder.

He promptly cut off her shriek with a callused hand clamped over her mouth. His steely arm pinned hers to her side and pressed her body against his chest. She writhed and shook, trying to free herself, but the wall of muscle at her back didn't even seem to register her struggle. Her frantic effort only made her lungs burn for the oxygen he was depriving her of.

When her head began spinning in earnest, her muscles went limp and her fight ebbed away.

Only then did she realize that the man was speaking softly in her ear, his whispered breath fanning the trembling muscles of her neck.

"Jess, calm down. I won't hurt you." The words made no sense to her muddled brain, but they continued, quiet and assured. "Don't scream. It's all right. I won't let anything happen to you."

It wasn't the words that made her sink into him, but the voice that, even after all this time, she'd recognize anywhere. Her eyes hadn't been playing tricks on her that afternoon. Will Gumble was in this compound. In her very room.

He must have sensed her acquiescence. He

slowly loosened his hand from over her mouth and rested it on her upper arm. His firm grip was the only thing that kept her standing.

"What are you—" Her words were little more than a frantic sigh as he spun her around. Pressing one finger to his lips, he raised his eyebrows and nodded toward the only other door in the room.

He didn't wait for her to agree, just steered her toward the bathroom and closed the door behind them.

She yanked on the string above the sink, and the naked bulb over the cloudy mirror burst to life, bathing them in its yellow glow. Jess blinked against the sudden brightness.

Will didn't seem to have the same trouble. He immediately lifted the lid off the toilet tank and peered inside before running his hands under the white porcelain sink. With a finger he swiped around the edge of the mirror. Then he leaned forward until her nose was almost pressed to his chest, and he swiped his hand over the top of the door frame.

He pulled back and nodded, as if satisfied. "It's clear. There may be bugs in your room, so we should never talk in there. But this should be safe for now."

Scrambling to catch up to his train of thought, Jess surveyed the sink and mirror. How could he act so casual? As if it hadn't been ten years since they'd spoken? As if he hadn't just shown up in a foreign country where she was being held prisoner? As if the very sight of him didn't make her knees weak with relief?

"I thought I saw you—I thought that was you, but…" Her words were little more than a whisper despite his assurance that it was safe to speak. Her stomach pitched, fear and relief mingling with alarm and the echo of a remembered betrayal. But dealing with her emotions would have to wait until she felt steadier on her feet. Exhaustion and the ebbing of her fight-or-flight adrenaline rush had left her legs like jelly. She leaned into Will. He held out his arms, as though he knew just what she needed. As though he was still someone who cared about taking care of her, being there for her.

But she didn't want him holding her. She wanted answers. She wanted to understand what on earth was happening. Most of all, she wanted to silence the little voice in her head that kept saying Will's appearance was simply a dream or hallucination.

Yanking herself upright at the last possible moment, she shoved his chest with both hands. "You scared me to death! Why did you break into my room? What are you doing here?"

His lopsided grin had always started with a

little quirk to the left before spreading across his mouth. And that hadn't changed, even as he looked down at the tiny black-and-white-checkered floor tiles.

He scraped his fingers over the black whiskers covering his chin. "Your dad sent me."

"My dad?"

"Well, I couldn't say no to my new XO, could I?"

"So you're still in the navy?" Oh, she sounded bitter—so much more bitter than she wanted to. Why couldn't her words be flippant and nonchalant, as if it didn't really matter that she no longer knew even the most basic things about him? He'd popped back into her life, and she didn't want it to matter.

But it did.

Maybe because of the extreme situation.

Sure. She'd just keep telling herself that.

His smile flickered for a moment before he nodded slowly. "I am."

Forcing a chuckle, she said, "I figured when my dad realized I was missing, he'd send a SEAL team to bring me home." At least she had hoped he'd do that.

"Not a full team—he just sent one."

Her breath vanished, and she blinked twice.

Will Gumble had become a SEAL. An elite

warrior. The best that the United States military offered.

What else didn't she know about him?

Will crossed his arms over his chest. Anything to keep from reaching out for Jess again. From being rejected again.

But he couldn't pull his gaze from her face, all smooth lines and fair skin, except for the dark bags below her bloodshot eyes. Those were both probably recent additions. Most people couldn't sleep much under this kind of stress. Just because he'd been trained to survive for days on catnaps didn't mean Jess would look refreshed doing the same.

Her hair brushed across her forehead and her eyebrows pulled together, leaving three vertical lines in the center.

"Where's the rest of your team?"

"Stateside."

With stilted movements, she crossed her arms, matching his stance. Her gaze swept from his head to his toes and back again, her eyes shifting from pale green to the color of the sea in a typhoon. The scrutiny made him feel like a kid who'd been called into the principal's office.

He resisted the sudden urge to flex his arms against the seams in the sport coat to remind her that he wasn't a boy any longer. This wasn't about how much either one of them had changed. This was about getting her—and her bioweapon—back to San Diego. Back to a lab where they would both be secure.

"Why'd you come alone? Don't you usually stick together?"

He lifted one shoulder. "Usually. But this isn't exactly an authorized op."

The corners of her mouth turned down, confusion washing across her features. "What does that mean?"

"I'm…freelancing."

"So my dad just asked you to rescue me, even though we haven't seen each other since we were eighteen? He asked you to drop everything and come to…to—" she waved her hand toward the yellowing walls "—wherever we are?" She paused, staring hard into his eyes. "And you did?"

For the first time in years, he didn't know what to say, so he spit out the only word that came to mind. *"Panama."*

"What?"

"We're in Panama."

She clenched her slightly crooked teeth and shook her head, long brown locks falling over her shoulders. "That's not— I didn't mean… We're in Panama? No, that's not what… Why are you here?" Her words were a jumbled mess, and ended in a weary sigh. Not harsh, just confused.

Truthfully, he wasn't sure how to answer. But she deserved something more than a pat response. Taking a deep breath, he let it out through his nose before offering her what he hoped was a white-flag smile. "We were friends once. You meant a lot to me."

"But you disappeared. You never called or responded to my emails or even came back to visit. I had to find out from your mom that you'd joined the navy." Her voice picked up volume as memories seemed to fuel her ire, and he pressed a finger to his lips. She immediately dropped her volume, but she couldn't hide the vibrato of her voice. "You left, and suddenly you're back when I need someone the most? I don't understand." Her hands shook and her eyes glistened as her emotions jumped to the forefront.

True. Everything she'd said was true, but this wasn't the time to rehash his immature stupidity. They needed to make a plan, but he had a feeling she was too exhausted to think tactically. That was fine—he needed at least a day to get the lay of the land, anyway. And meanwhile, she needed sleep and to know she was safe enough to truly give in to it.

"Jess, I'm sorry. You're right. I do owe you an explanation. But maybe that can wait. For now, can you trust me enough to believe that I will find a way to get you out of here?"

"And the Morsyni powder?"

"Yes. I'll get you both out."

The features of her face were still pinched as she pointed toward the outside wall. "How? You can't exactly climb over that fence. And there are guards everywhere. How are you going to get us out of here?"

"I'm not sure yet. But I'll come up with something. Just give me some time."

Her eyes grew wide. "We don't have time. I don't know what they're planning to do with the toxin, but it's going to happen soon. All day my guard has been muttering to himself that he only has to deal with me for eight more days. I think they brought me here to release the Morsyni. What if they get impatient? What if we don't even have that long?"

A slow grin spread across his face, and she stopped her frantic speech. "What are you smiling about?" she demanded.

"Nothing." But it wasn't nothing. Jess had said *we.* She was going to stick with him. She trusted him enough to think of them as a team. And the rest of the trust he had to earn back…well, that would come with time. "I will find a way out, all right? And until then, I'm going to be by your side as much as possible. You just have to pretend that you don't know me."

She uncrossed her arms and leaned against the

sink, her palms resting on the lip of porcelain. It looked as if it took all of her strength to stay on her feet. "Why?"

"The powers that be inside this drug cartel think they brought me here to help you release a bioweapon. They think I'm an engineer."

"But you're not, are you? What do you know about science?"

"About as much as I picked up in our sopho-more-year chemistry class."

"So why do they think you can help me?" She squinted, the turning cogs in her mind nearly visible beneath the fair skin of her forehead.

"A friend of mine in the DEA used one of her undercover contacts to spread my name—well, the name William Darrow—around as an expert on Morsyni, and this cartel took the bait. They hauled me in—just like they did you."

She blinked fast, pressing a palm against her forehead and swaying slightly. It was a lot of information to take in at one time. A lot to think about on severely limited sleep. He got that. "So we don't know each other," she finally said.

"Right. They're going to drag me to your lab tomorrow and introduce us. I need you to act like you've never met me before in your life."

"All right."

He rubbed his palm up and down her arm,

either to steady her swaying form or to see if this time she'd accept his touch, his comfort.

Definitely the first.

Probably.

No, it had to be the first because there could never be anything more than friendship between them.

"We've got to stay under the radar and keep the guards off our scent," he said. "Can you help me maintain my cover until we get out of the country?"

"Panama." Her tongue slurred the word, her eyes squinting into the space over his left shoulder.

"Right." With a gentle hand, he held on to her elbow, keeping her upright. Some of the tension in her face eased, and she leaned toward him slightly. "You need to get some sleep," he said. "Tomorrow we'll try to work out a plan."

"What kind of plan?"

Will glanced toward the ceiling, hoping to find answers there. But all he discovered were big patches of green mold marring the once white tiles. For a multimillion-dollar drug lord, whoever was running this cartel sure had let his compound fall into disrepair.

"Probably something like tonight. I'll break into your room and we'll get out of here." He rubbed his shoulder, which would have a bruise the next day. In a lighter tone, he added, "Maybe next time try not to hit me with your wrench."

The teasing was lost on her, but she nodded.

"Listen, when we leave here, I need you to have the strength to run and the presence of mind to think on your feet. This sleepwalking bit you're pulling isn't going to cut it. You've got to get some rest."

Her eyes flew wide open, her head whipping from side to side. "I can't."

"Why not?" As soon as the words left his mouth, he recognized his stupidity. She'd been waiting for him, weapon in hand, when he'd crept into her room. She had been prepared for anyone.

Because it might not be him sneaking into her room.

His stomach rolled at the thought, bile rising in the back of his throat.

He squinted at her, trying to guess what she'd endured at the hands of these monsters. Her guard had laughed at her when she'd fallen into the mud that afternoon. How much worse had it been? Will tightened his grip on her elbow, but she didn't shy away, instead leaning more heavily against him. "Have you been— Has there been—" Words failed him at first, but he pushed on. "Has someone else come in here?"

She gave an almost imperceptible shake of her

head. "Not yet." Her voice had barely enough force to reach his ears.

A rock fell in his gut, thudding heavily. "But they've threatened to?"

"It's more the leers and foul gestures. And the noises late at night. You know what I mean?"

He nodded because he didn't want to hear the tremble in her voice for another second. Some men—twisted men—took pleasure in frightening and harming women.

Those men made Will sick.

Others were just too self-centered to notice a woman's discomfort in the face of crudeness.

And Will knew a thing or two about the latter. At some point in history, sailors had earned a reputation for language and conduct unbecoming of gentlemen. And there was still a group of them determined to carry on that tradition. He'd even been one of them when he'd first joined up. Too arrogant to recognize his own impudence.

But that was before he'd met L. T. Sawyer, Rock Waterstone, Jordan Somerton and the other men of SEAL Team Fifteen. Before he'd joined their ranks.

Will wasn't that cocky boy any longer. And he would do whatever it took to protect Jess.

Stabbing his fingers through his hair, he snatched several quick breaths. His pulse slowed to almost normal when he closed his eyes and forced himself not to think about Jess in jeopardy.

"Here's what we're going to do. I'm going to make sure that you're safe. Every night."

Drooping eyelids lifted with hope, but uncertainty still masked her face. "How?" she asked.

"I'll be right outside your door from midnight until the first movement in the morning. I won't let anyone near you."

She wanted to believe him. He could see it in her eyes.

But she wouldn't forget that he'd once let her down. That he'd once promised to come back and hadn't followed through.

How could he convince her that he wouldn't do that again?

Cupping her cheek with his palm, he brushed his thumb over her cheekbone. "I never stopped being your friend. I just didn't know how to be your best friend when everything was changing. But I swear to you, I'll be here to protect you until you're safely back in San Diego. In time for Christmas. All right?"

She swallowed, her head lowering and lifting slowly.

It was all he needed before he turned off the light and whisked her back into her bedroom. She fell onto the mattress, her head landing on a thin pillow. By the time he pulled a thread-bare blanket to her shoulders, her breathing had already slowed.

"How's Sal?"

Her voice caught him halfway to the door, but it was what she said that stopped him short. A fist around his throat choked his response, and he had to cough before he could even whisper. "He's fine. He misses you, I think. But he's fine."

"Is he married?"

The fingers around Will's neck squeezed even tighter, until his response was little more than a breath. "No." He didn't expound. Couldn't manage to tell her that his brother was still hung up on her after all these years.

Instead he closed the door behind him and slipped around the side of the small building. Tucked in the shadows, out of sight of the guards standing sentry over the compound walls, he squatted, ready to wait the night through. At least he'd have some time to formulate a plan to keep a madman from releasing the deadly bioweapon. Right now the best option looked as if it would involve some kind of escape.

But Will wouldn't be able to walk Jess out the front gate. And they had to get away without the extraction services of the United States Navy. There was a lot of land between them and the American Embassy in Panama City. A lot of cartel-controlled land.

This was a foolhardy idea.

And there was nothing he'd rather do.

THREE

Jess glanced at the heavy metal door—the only entrance to her lab—again. Still no sign of her new lab mate. Manuel, however, leaned on the doorjamb, one hand in his pocket, the other resting loosely on the black machine gun hanging from its strap on his shoulder. A black gas mask hung around his neck. Jess didn't bother to tell him it was outdated and probably wouldn't protect him from the toxin contained in a plastic vial.

At least it was a sight better than the paper mask they'd given her. If they expected her to open the airtight canister containing the toxin, they'd have to give her better protective gear. At her lab back home, she'd had a full-body suit and her own oxygen supply inside a lab with double air locks.

Clearly, her hosts in Panama didn't care if she lived or died. They were just concerned with finding a way to disperse the small quantity of Morsyni over a wide area. Whoever the target was, she felt sorry for them. The effects of the toxin would be widespread and instantaneous, causing painful sores on the skin and even worse abrasions on the lungs. The airborne pathogen wouldn't cause immediate death, rather its fingers would slowly constrict the lungs until they could inhale no more painful breaths.

"Aye!" Manuel's shrill call told her that his relaxed pose was only a facade. Apparently, she wasn't unloading and cleaning the box of scientific instruments fast enough for him.

"Time. It takes time."

"No time. Now."

Why? Why did it have to be done now? She bit her tongue before the words could escape. He only got angry when she asked him questions. She cranked up a Bunsen burner and set a beaker of water to boil, dropping in an unmeasured mound of NaCl, sodium chloride, better known as common table salt. Maybe that would buy her some time. At least she looked busy, and the swirling mist of dissolving salt gave Manuel something to focus on while she unpacked microscope slides and set about washing them.

And considered her options.

If she really wanted to release the toxin in aerosol form in this sort of lab, her best option would be to disassemble used tear gas canisters and repurpose them.

But she didn't want to release it. She wanted to destroy it. Except there wasn't a way to destroy the powder without releasing the ultramicroscopic spores into the air. The lab didn't have a detonation chamber, and the ventilation hood in the back corner wasn't capable of containing such an acute toxin. Her best chance was to escape before the toxin was scheduled to be released, with the powder in hand. But could she keep stalling until Will found them a way out?

Her stomach jumped at the memory of her midnight visitor. She'd been safe. If just for a few hours before he'd knocked softly on her window to wake her before leaving his self-assigned post, she'd rested. That morning her mind hadn't been blank, her muscles not quite so sluggish.

Will had protected her for the night. But could he keep it up until they found an escape?

Three loud thumps sounded on the metal door, jerking Jess from her thoughts.

"Safe?" Hampered by lack of English, Manuel asked with his eyes what he couldn't express in words. If he allowed any toxin out into the compound, he would be dead before the Morsyni could take effect.

She nodded. *"Sí."*

He cocked his head, as if to confirm her certainty, and she nodded again.

The natural brilliance of the sun streaming

through the open door blinded her after a morning under the painful glow of flickering fluorescent lights. Blinking into it, she could make out two forms. The easy swagger and relaxed movements of the larger man overshadowed the silhouette at his side.

The door's heavy metal clawed against cement before clanging shut and leaving the brilliance on the other side.

The first man wore a brown military uniform, the buttons straining against his belly. The hunched shoulders and wary stance of the figure at his side practically made the smaller man disappear into the other's shadow.

Will stood there with all the presence of a sea monkey.

Jess clenched her jaw to keep her mouth from falling open. This man, this fragment of a figure, was not the same one who had broken into her room the night before. He looked beaten. He'd been bested.

Whatever they'd done to him…

Her imagination shot to the worst possible scenario. If they'd found him sneaking back into his room, they wouldn't have gently escorted him out of the compound. They'd have used their fists and feet or worse to make him do whatever they wanted.

The night before, he'd been so strong, had filled her room with such power.

He'd looked the part of a SEAL.

But not now.

It took everything inside her not to run to him, wrap her arm around his slumped shoulders and ask if he was seriously injured.

And then he caught her gaze with his own. And he winked.

She sucked in a quick breath, the air catching in her throat, tearing a cough from somewhere deep in her chest.

He was playing a part. *The* part. She should have realized that the cartel wouldn't have believed the man in her room the night before was a scientist. That man was a battle-tested, steely-eyed warrior. And he had nothing in common with the figure standing before her now.

Straightening her shoulders, she blinked away the rush of relief, focusing hard on the boiling salt water on the burner.

Will's guard shoved him hard, and he stumbled—convincingly—into the corner of the table. His grunt echoed and was only drowned out by the yell of Manuel's partner in crime. Spanish words poured from his mouth faster than she could understand them, but he jabbed the barrel of his gun in her direction.

Stomach turning to steel, she was suddenly

unable to move as the round end of the weapon filled her field of vision. She heard Will's shuffling feet move in her direction until she was suddenly staring at his back. He held up appeasing hands and nodded slowly. *"Sí,"* he mumbled, his voice sounding pained and unfamiliar. "Whatever you say. Yes. *Sí.*"

Why was his Spanish so awkward? It didn't make any sense. She knew that he spoke Spanish fluently. He and Sal both had learned from their mother's mother—their *abuelita*—who had lived with the family for years.

The guard grumbled something else, and Will just kept nodding and agreeing in a jumbled mix of Spanish and English words until the other man marched toward the door, his footfalls ringing into every corner of the cement bunker.

Will turned his back to their guards. He offered her a flash of a smile and mouthed, *Okay?*

She gave a quick nod of her head.

"They want us to work together." His voice was barely audible, and she leaned into him, resting her hand on his forearm, to catch the words. "Your guy is mad about what they're having for lunch, so he's going to leave early to try to sneak some leftovers from the cook."

Suddenly she realized what was going on. Will's awkwardness with the language was entirely an act. It was all for show, so he could listen in on what the guards were saying without them realizing he understood every word.

It was a smart tactic. But like everything else that had happened since his arrival the previous day, it threw her for a loop.

Her pulse kicked into high gear. She was supposed to pretend she didn't know him. She had to act as if she'd never seen him before. She needed everyone else in the compound to believe that Will Gumble hadn't been the only person keeping her sane when her father had deployed, for the millionth time, during her sophomore year, and she'd been left again with her great-aunt.

That was the same year they'd both been in the high school drama team's production of *My Fair Lady*. Maybe Will didn't remember that she'd been dropped from the program for missing cues and flubbing lines.

She couldn't do this. She was going to mess it up and get them both killed.

Sweat peppered her palms, and she wiped them against her pants beneath the canvas chemistry apron.

"It's all right."

Will's face was so calm, his smile so easy, she could almost believe they weren't in any real danger. Until she glanced past him toward the two men standing watch at the door. "How can you say that?"

"Because we're in this together."

She jumped at the implied camaraderie. Deep in her heart, she wanted to believe him, but it wasn't quite that easy. They'd been together when her father, then a commander, had deployed. They'd been together the summer she'd spent praying her mother would come back. They'd been together when her great-aunt had taken a nasty fall and broken her hip. But when Sal offered her a promise ring, Will had flat-out disappeared. Ten years of silence, and she was supposed to trust him again?

She glanced toward the door as Manuel's voice grew animated and he gestured wildly to his friend, their attention clearly not on their charges. Manuel was probably still thinking about his lunch.

Whether he could read the doubt on her face or sense the tension in her shaking fists, Will's smile dipped. "Why don't you give me a tour of the lab? What are you working on?" He inclined his head toward her beaker, sounding sincerely interested.

"Boiling some water." Oh, why had she said that? What if the guards overheard? Her chest tightened, a hiccup popping out before she could stop it. When her stomach pinched in nervous knots, she always ended up with the hiccups.

Clapping a hand over her mouth, she squeezed her eyes shut and prayed that the hiccups would stop.

Will took a step, drawing close enough that his heat tickled her arms, and she let out another hiccup.

He was *not* helping the situation.

"Aye! Work!" Manuel yelled, his gun pointing toward the ceiling above their heads. He spit out a string of Spanish before jerking his head back to his friend.

Will nodded toward the black supply cabinet in the rear of the room. "Maybe you should show me around."

Will peered over Jess's shoulder into the dim confines of the locker along the back wall. Rows of glass beakers, plastic tubing and other basic chemistry items lined the shelves. But even he could tell the lab as a whole was ill equipped to handle the kind of science that Jess had been doing back in San Diego. It was probably more accustomed to housing meth mixers than biological weapons.

A refrigerated locker sat on the counter right next to the cupboard. Its sides were stainless steel, but the door on top was made of a clear Plexiglas. And a three-inch padlock kept the curious from opening it.

"That's it." She pointed toward the top of the

fridge and a small black cube inside that boasted a yellow biohazard sticker. The lid was locked in place with four clamps, maintaining the airtight seal. The whole thing wasn't much bigger than his fist, but the way she gave it a wide berth suggested its size didn't have a direct correlation to its power.

"That's the toxin?"

"Morsyni." Her tone carried no small amount of reverence and a slight quiver of fear.

He caught her gaze and held it, dropping his voice low. "What is it? What exactly can it do?"

The muscles at her throat constricted as a flicker passed through her eyes. "What's in that case is enough to kill every person in San Diego and the rest of California. And we're not talking about an easy death."

As his stomach clenched, he shot a look at the guards to make sure they were still ignoring them. "How bad?"

"You've heard of botulism?"

He nodded. "Sure. It causes trouble breathing and paralysis."

"Usually. And it can also result in severe internal distress. Its root is the botulinum toxin, which causes nerve damage."

He pointed at the black box. "Is that what's in there?"

Jess shook her head, her long, dark ponytail

swishing over her shoulders. "The effects of the Morsyni toxin are sometimes called botulism two point oh."

"So if it's released, it'll kill everyone in the area."

"An ugly, painful death." She finally glanced away, dropping her gaze to her clasped hands. "For all of us."

He sucked in the suddenly thick air. It had been humid all morning, but now he felt as if he was trying to catch a deep breath at the bottom of a pool.

The two men at the door grew louder, an argument erupting between them about who was going to go get lunch first. Sergio, the one who had been shoving Will around the compound, yanked on the door handle and marched past Manuel, who stuck his boot out, tripping his comrade. Manuel received a hard knock on the leg in retaliation.

As the men tussled, Will slowly stepped in front of Jess, blocking their view of her. She pressed a palm to his arm and whispered against his back, "What's going on?"

Over his shoulder he replied in an equally low tone, "They're both hungry. Best to look busy and stay out of their line of sight. One of them is going to lose this fight, and he won't be happy about it."

Jess nodded, pulling on a pair of rubber gloves

and picking up metal tongs. Her movements were stilted and jerky, but productive, as she emptied and cleaned the beaker she'd been boiling water in.

While she worked and the guards continued to argue, Will slipped silently along the back wall, his hands roaming over the uneven cinder blocks. Just to the left of the supply cabinet, a dingy, yellowed window overlooked the security wall, sparks of sunlight reflecting off of the jagged edges of green and brown glass standing sentry along its top.

With a quick survey around the edges of the window, he confirmed that despite its age and color, it appeared solid. Unfortunately, he couldn't jump onto the counter to get a closer look. At least not right that moment.

The only other window in the room was a rectangle even with the top of the door on the front wall. It contained a sputtering air conditioner, which worked about as well as a drop of water fighting a wildfire. It couldn't possibly keep up with the jungle's humidity, but at least the limited natural light in the building also blocked most of the force of the sun.

The window along the back wall was the only one that could possibly be useful for an escape. Or a break-in. But given the containment storage it required, most likely the toxin was going to have to come with them through the rusty metal door or be left behind.

And Jess had made it clear that the latter wasn't an option.

Manuel and Sergio's row reached its apex, and Will glanced at Jess, whose eyes were wide in her pale face. Checking to make sure that the guards were still not paying attention, he sidled up to her, rolling up his white shirtsleeves before slipping one of the black aprons off the hook on the wall, pulling it over his head and tying it into place on top of his wrinkled button-up.

"They've moved on from lunch. Now they're arguing about which one will have the more important role in something that's happening in a week."

"Seriously?" The tension that wrinkled her forehead grew tighter. "What's going to happen?"

He began to answer, but before he could speak the commotion suddenly and abruptly ceased, leaving the air thick with only the choked coughs coming from the air-conditioning unit. Will slammed his mouth closed and slipped Jess behind him as a third man joined the guards. Manuel sucked in his stomach and pushed out his chest, his arms holding his M6 at a perfect forty-five degree angle. Sergio snapped to attention, too—though his presentation wasn't quite as smooth.

The stranger was a short man with slicked-back hair and a long mustache that curled over his upper lip. He clasped his hands behind his back, his eyes sweeping over the men, who clearly reported to him.

"El Jefe," Manuel said.

The boss. This man was either the kingpin or someone important enough to speak in the cartel leader's stead.

Sergio didn't address El Jefe, but his eyes dropped to the rough cement floor, his grip on his weapon tightening until his fingers turned white. The boss clearly commanded respect, and he didn't bother with more than a glance in Will and Jess's direction.

"Cuando va a estar listo?" The mustache flipped toward the back of the lab, toward them.

Manuel mumbled something that Will couldn't make out, and a fist tightened at the back of his shirt as Jess twisted the fabric and leaned into him. She didn't have to ask her question for him to know that she wanted him to translate. But she was going to have to wait. He couldn't afford to reveal that he understood everything they were saying.

Not yet, anyway.

The boss growled in response to Manuel's answer, pressing fingers like round sausages into his hips at his belt. Then he let loose a stream of curses intermingled with enough information to set Will's heart beating faster than a chopper blade. *"Siete días. Entiendes?"*

Then he stomped away, leaving Sergio and Manuel to return to their bitter words, angry glares and childish fighting.

"What's going on?"

Will felt more than heard Jess's words, and turned back to her, his arms and legs already beginning to tingle with pent-up energy.

"That man is in charge while Juan Carlos, the kingpin, is away. But Juan Carlos is coming back, and when he does, they're going to release the toxin at a party at a nearby cartel."

Jess's eyes grew wide again, and she gasped, biting down on the sound to keep from alerting their guards. "When will he be here?"

"Seven days." Will leaned down until they were eye to eye, and whispered, "We—and the toxin—have to be out of here in six."

FOUR

Jess jumped, instantly alert, at the two quick taps on her window. It was Will's sign that the sun was about to rise, and he had to get back to his own cell.

Rolling from her bed, she stumbled to the wall below the windowpane and stretched to respond with three raps of her own. One more knock from him signaled his farewell.

She stifled a yawn as she plopped back down onto the lumpy mattress, ignoring the way the springs below it poked through the tattered fabric. She had been given the luxury of only a single blanket, and 600-thread-count sheets seemed a dream from another lifetime. Still, she'd never felt more rested.

Maybe it was just the comparison to every other morning since she'd been abducted, but five whole hours of uninterrupted sleep felt positively decadent.

She was tempted to lie back down, but instead

stood and wandered toward the bathroom. After splashing cold water on her face and combing her wild bed head, she felt more like her old self—her San Diego self.

Strange. Nothing was really different. In the five days she'd spent in this compound, her schedule, guard and job had remained the same. Nothing had changed.

Except Will's arrival.

A pounding on the door preceded the click of the lock, and she turned to meet Manuel in the middle of the room. His face contorted when she appeared, his frown turning even more sour. Lemons were sweeter than his scowl.

She considered giving him a smile, just to see how he'd react, until he waved his giant black machine gun toward her middle. *"Vámanos."*

No amount of sleep made looking down the barrel of a gun more tolerable, so she simply nodded and trudged toward the door, trying to keep Manuel in her peripheral vision. His stride kept him about half a step behind her, but she didn't need to see him to feel the weight of his breath muss the hair on the back of her head.

She picked up her pace, but he matched her movements even as she cringed away from his presence. Five hours without worry, five hours without vigilance, and she'd clearly forgotten the oppression of the man who shadowed her every move. But now she couldn't shake him.

Her steps carried them past more than a dozen other cinder block buildings haloed by the morning sun. All just like hers, except for the absence of locks on the wooden doors.

They finally reached the mess hall, a single room filled with a dozen long, shallow tables. The far corner hosted a kitchen with stainless steel griddles that looked more suited for a food truck than a drug cartel's fine dining establishment. Maybe they'd had some lean years. Or maybe the kitchen wasn't their priority.

A lone man in a stained apron stood over one griddle, slinging fried potatoes with a metal spatula that could have easily served as a machete in the surrounding jungle. He lifted his hand and hollered a greeting that she'd come to recognize meant that she should grab a plate—the cleanest one she could find—and bring it over for her meager allotment of morning foodstuffs.

"Buenos días." His words rolled as fast as his hand flung the sizzling chorizo across the greasy metal stove top. While he didn't look up from his task, it was clear that his verbal greeting wasn't directed at her, and Manuel grunted a somewhat less intelligible response.

Jess picked up a sand-colored plastic plate. The chef didn't even wait for her to extend her dish before slopping half a day's worth of calories toward the front of her shirt. Flying sausage and potatoes arced right for her chest. Throwing up her plate as a shield, she ducked.

A shove on her shoulder propelled her off balance. The toe of her shoe caught on a crack in the floor. She stumbled toward Manuel, who jumped out of her way, leaving her to crash against the cement wall.

But a jerk at her elbow caught her just before she fell. In one fluid motion, she spun around, the soles of her Converse sneakers finding purchase just as her gaze met Will's reserved stare. He looked at the mess on the floor as his fingers loosened from her arm one at a time, making sure she was really stable before fully releasing her.

"Pardon me." His ludicrously long eyelashes flickered as he backed away, refusing to meet her stare again.

Their guards bellowed at the same time, and Sergio's fleshy fist came down on Will's shoulder—right where Jess had hit him with the wrench a few nights before. With pinched lips and squinting eyes, Will looked behind him and mumbled an apology. The pain looked real, and it probably was.

But its effects were exaggerated. They had to be.

Will had made it through Hell Week—the most

taxing training in the already intense SEAL regimen. He wouldn't crumble under the pressure of a Panamanian drug thug.

The cook glared between the mess at his feet and Jess's still outstretched plate. He pointed at the floor, rattling off something in Spanish so fast she couldn't understand. But Manuel stepped in, saying there was no time. Probably for her to clean up the mess.

With a string of expletives, the cook slopped a spoonful of breakfast on her plate before Manuel pushed her to the corner table, and Will joined her a moment later.

But this was no leisurely meal. The two guards stood with crossed arms, watching every move Jess and Will made. She shoveled down the food so fast that she barely tasted it, except for the lingering fire of the spicy sausage.

Suddenly Sergio pulled on the back of Will's shirt, tugging him out of the chair and toward the exit.

Eager to keep Manuel's hands off her, Jess hopped to her feet and chased after Will, leaving several bites left on her plate.

Will fell into step beside her as they ambled across the muddy yard, their guards several paces behind.

"I'm sorry." Her words were barely loud enough to make it to his ear.

He raised one eyebrow in a signature questioning glance.

"That breakfast was rushed." Will hadn't had time to finish his serving, either.

Nothing about his posture or gait changed, and she felt more than heard his response. "I've survived on less before."

What was that supposed to mean? He'd always had plenty. While not rich, his parents had owned a modest home in a nice neighborhood, only a few blocks from the house she'd shared with Great-aunt Eva after her mother had packed up everything she valued in two suitcases and walked out of Jess's life forever.

Will's grandmother had kept them all stuffed. Huevos rancheros and beans. Handmade corn tortillas and carne asada. Tamales and *muchaca*. The whole family—Will and Sal, aunts and uncles, cousins—had squeezed in around a table and feasted on Abuelita's specialties. And at least once a week during high school, Jess had pulled up a chair between the two brothers and downed chile relleno as if she hadn't eaten a home-cooked meal since she was twelve years old.

And that was really only partially true.

Her father had learned to cook, and when he wasn't on a ship in waters unknown, his table had been set with better-than-edible pot roast. When he was deployed and Great-aunt Eva came to stay in her home, Jess ate with the Gumbles.

She had firsthand evidence that Will had never gone hungry.

A glance to her right confirmed that their guards were still deep in conversation as they trudged toward the big house and the shed beyond, so she shot Will a questioning glare. "What do you mean?" Her words were barely a hiss, and she hadn't anticipated a deep rumble and high-pitched shouting that caught everyone's attention.

They all spun toward the daunting steel gates below a stucco arch. Two men on either side leaned their shoulders against the metal and shoved, grunting until the wheels at their feet budged.

Will threw a protective arm in front of Jess and she hopped back three steps, as two covered military transport vehicles squeezed through the opening, rolled across the courtyard and stopped just to the right of the big house.

Weapons bouncing across their chests, Manuel and Sergio jogged over to greet the drivers, clapping their backs, then peering over the tailgates at whatever bounty the trucks carried.

Jess glanced up at Will, whose eyes had narrowed in on the reunion. He remained impossibly still, and she almost missed his quiet words.

"They're going to unload the trucks this afternoon, and they'll leave early in the morning."

"How do you—" She stopped herself as a muscle in his neck jumped, his jaw clenching as his eyes followed the back-and-forth shouts of the men.

"They're going to get drunk this afternoon, sleep it off and go wheels-up before first light." Again he gave no outward indication that he was speaking to her, but his voice rang with something akin to excitement. It wasn't loud or boisterous, just filled with anticipation.

She tried to make her body mimic his ease, but her hands fluttered aimlessly as she tried to find a natural-looking pose. Finally she shoved them into her pockets and refused to let go of the fabric there. "What are they carrying?"

His deep brown eyes shifted toward her. "It doesn't really matter what they have now. When they leave, they'll be taking us with them."

"How are we going to get on those trucks?"

At the squeak of Jess's voice, Will forced himself to stay still, leaving his hands and arms hanging loosely at his sides. The weight of her gaze was heavier than a flak jacket, but he schooled his features, once again looking aloof and perhaps even disinterested. If they were going to make it on one of those trucks, they couldn't afford to draw any extra attention from the guards. Not Manuel and Sergio, and certainly not the line of men strolling near the front gate, their semi-automatics resting too comfortably against their shoulders.

Jess must have picked up on his stance, for her shoulders relaxed a fraction and she took a deep breath through her nose.

"We won't leave without the toxin." Only the left side of her mouth moved, and if he hadn't been so close, he would have missed her words. "Right?"

"I promised, didn't I?"

"Yes, well…" Her clipped words nearly dripped icicles in the jungle. "Your promises haven't always meant much."

He deserved that. Absolutely. But he'd hoped that maybe she'd forgotten his last broken promise. Or at least that she'd put aside her hostility long enough for them to get beyond these walls and to the United States Embassy in Panama City.

Really, he thought they'd been doing fairly well. After all, she'd slept while he guarded her door. He could tell just by the thinning of the bags beneath her eyes. And she'd agreed to pretend she didn't know him. She'd done a fine job playing the part. So why the terse words now?

His stomach rumbled, calling out for some of

the spilled breakfast they'd both been forced to skimp on.

Maybe he wasn't the only one wishing they hadn't left behind half of their meals.

Hunger had always made Jess a little bit ornery.

He reminded himself that it wasn't her fault that he'd proved himself untrustworthy. He'd promised to pick her up, and he hadn't. Instead he'd disappeared. Completely vanished from her life. It had just been so much easier than facing pain he couldn't explain and fear he didn't fully understand.

Sal had given Jess a promise ring, and Will had given her broken promises.

If anyone else had proposed to Jess, Will would have figured out a way to voice the turmoil that warred inside of him at the very thought of losing her. On their last night together, so many years ago, he would have spoken up and told her the truth. He might have been too young and foolish to put a voice to exactly how he felt about her, but he'd have done anything to keep her in his life.

Anything except betraying Sal.

His only brother. His oldest friend. His rescuer.

Almost ten months before he proposed to Jess, Sal had single-handedly saved Will from a senior year of misery and regret.

With one word—one sacrifice—Sal gave up his freedom for Will's. Whatever distance the years had placed between them, Will wouldn't forget that.

He'd known ten years ago that he couldn't step on his brother's chance for happiness, so he'd done the only thing he knew to do. He had run.

That wasn't Jess's fault.

It wasn't her fault, either, that she wasn't around when he'd gotten his life on track. When L.T. and Rock had convinced him that being a man of honor and faith was better than carousing through San Diego bars. When he'd taken their encouragement and used it to propel himself through BUD/S training. When he'd received his trident pin, become a SEAL. A man of valor.

As Sergio marched toward them, his mouth twisted in an angry scowl, Will knew there wasn't time to tell her the whole story, even if she was willing to hear him out.

Taking a deep breath, he whispered only what he could promise her in that moment. "You can trust me now."

Fire in her eyes said she didn't entirely believe him, but it disappeared immediately and she turned an indifferent expression on their guards, who yelled for them to change direction and march toward the lab. Will fell into a shuffling step beside Jess, his feet dragging through the brown puddles that dotted the courtyard. Her pace quickly outstripped his, and he thought she was going to abandon him to the sour-faced guards. Just as she reached the point where slowing down to walk with him again would have been overly obvious, her shoulders relaxed. Taking three small steps, she let him catch up without drawing undo attention.

He gave her a silent nod, and she pinched her lips into a straight line, clearly not convinced that she should get on a transport with him to only God knew where.

He couldn't blame her.

But at the moment, it could be their only chance of escape, and he wasn't about to let it pass them by.

The inside of the lab was as visually cold as it was physically hot, and he glanced at the countertop refrigerator. At least it was still keeping the toxin cool and contained. Jess's gaze traveled in the same direction as though confirming that no one had tampered with the lethal powder during the night.

But if what she'd said about the Morsyni was true and someone had opened it in the dark hours, then none of them would have made it through the night.

Down the long alley between the barracks, back in front of the big house, the truck drivers were unloading their cargo with enough exuberance to draw the attention of every man in the area. Including Sergio and Manuel.

The lab door slammed as the guards went out to watch, leaving their two captives alone. Jess stared up at Will with unblinking eyes. Her pupils grew wider until they almost eclipsed the surrounding green, the questions there heavy and unspoken.

"We don't know if we're going to get another chance to escape," he whispered.

"Do you know where we are? Or what direction we need to go? Or even where the trucks are headed once they get beyond the wall?"

Her words rubbed at the same sore spot he'd been worrying since the trucks had rumbled through the gates.

"Not exactly." That was a partial truth at best. Honestly, he had no intel, no map, no communication with the outside world. Best-case scenario meant escaping on the truck, jumping off at an unknown location and humping into the jungle with nothing more than their clothes for cover and the stars to guide them.

The worst case meant a broken promise to not only Jess but also Captain McCoy.

But no matter how dangerous it would be to leave, it would be riskier to stay. Riskier for them, and for the thousands who would be killed if the drug lord had his way.

Jess rubbed her hands together before smoothing them over the counter, her gaze swinging around the work area as though she was looking for something—anything else—to focus on. "That wasn't very convincing."

He took a step closer to her, purposefully invading her space. Maybe then she'd look up at him and read his face and the truth there. He wouldn't let her down.

She didn't move.

Hunting for the words, Will took a long breath. "It's not the…ideal scenario." She grunted at his understatement. "But it's all we've got. I'd give my own truck for rations, a map of this area and an arrow pointing to Panama City. But there's no chance of getting any of those things."

Jabbing a finger toward the front of the compound, he continued. "Right now, we have a chance to get clear of that wall and away from these men, who I might remind you are planning on killing you and me, and plenty of other people, too. I'm not willing to risk your life on the chance that another opportunity and a map are going to show up in the next five days."

"You have a truck?"

Her change in topic nearly caused him whiplash.

She still didn't make eye contact, and her voice

stayed low as she added, "The red four-wheel drive you always wanted?"

"Why?"

Finally she looked up, and he could again read her thoughts clearly in her eyes.

Once, they'd been inseparable. She'd known him like no one else. She'd known his plans and ambitions—right down to the model and color of the truck he'd dreamed of buying. Now they were little more than strangers, and it felt like a knife wound to the stomach.

She hitched a breath and squinted until her nose wrinkled. "I was just wondering if maybe you're not so different from the boy I knew."

He couldn't tell her how much he hoped that wasn't true. He wasn't that stupid, selfish kid anymore.

And once he got her safely back to San Diego, maybe he could prove it to her. Maybe they could be friends again. Maybe they could resume some of that special bond they'd enjoyed.

Of course, it could never be just like it had been. He could never let himself get that close to her again. Even if she forgave him for disappearing, and wanted to spend hours together just talking. Even if he could explain why he'd had to leave. Even if she understood. Because if he let himself get close to her, he'd fall in love all over again.

And he'd never do that to Sal.

At the last family dinner Will had been able to attend, Sal had mentioned her. Just in passing, really. But the light in Sal's eyes at her memory had been brighter than a ship's beacon. His feelings were still strong.

Will wouldn't risk hurting his brother.

Something flickered in Jess's eyes just before she looked away, and he felt as if he'd lost his anchor.

Stepping back, he cleared his throat. "I'm not that same kid."

"I hope you're right." Her words were clipped, and her hands roamed the counter for something to keep her busy. She began unpacking the nearest box, stacking old tear gas canisters along the edge. "So when do we leave?"

"Be ready as soon as the compound goes to sleep."

She nodded as he slipped across the room, an eye always on the lab door. He picked up a jug of distilled water as though it was precious cargo, keeping his steps even and unhurried just in case their guards returned.

"What are you doing?" she murmured.

He nodded toward the window. "We have to have a way to get back in here tonight so we can retrieve the toxin." Will climbed onto the counter below the tiny glass pane, careful not to let his head reach above the sill in case someone was watching from the outside. Drawing suspicion meant drawing extra guards.

And they already had too many eyes following their every move.

With two fingers, he pressed on the window. It didn't budge, just like he'd thought. He added two more, pushing again. If he could just get it to rotate on its central hinge…but the thing probably hadn't been opened in ages—if ever. And years of jungle rains and splattering mud hadn't helped the situation. Making a fist, he used the edge of his hand to smack the base of the window.

It popped open with a creak just as the lab door swung into the room.

In one swift motion he dropped to the floor, snatched the water off the counter and walked toward the corner, where a five-gallon jug sat on a swiveling pedestal. Glancing up, he met Manuel's gaze as the guard sauntered inside, his eyes glinting with distrust above the red bandanna tied over his mouth and nose. His gas mask hung useless around his neck. The barrel of his ever-ready weapon flickered toward Will, as their eyes locked in a brief, wordless warning.

Will poured the distilled water into the larger container before ambling back toward Jess. Never once did he break eye contact with Manuel. It was out of character for the role Will played, but the tension in the guard's grip on the gun made the hair on Will's arms stand on end.

With an unhurried step, he slipped into place beside Jess, helping her unpack another box filled with a hodgepodge of equipment. But he didn't dare look down.

A sudden downpour struck their building as a jungle storm raged overhead. Sergio jumped into the room, swearing loudly and mumbling about how much he disliked his assignment and how much Juan Carlos was going to owe them when he got back.

The rain seemed insistent on getting inside, and Will shot a quick glance at the window he'd just opened. If it leaked and the guards noticed…

Jess's eyes followed his, and her lips turned white. Her nostrils flared, as if she was asking what he was going to do about it.

He nodded, brief and tight.

But there was no subtle way to close the window, so he set about pulling a rubber hose and more tear gas containers out of his box.

Jess's next box was filled with cleaning supplies, and when she was about halfway through emptying it, she glanced at the back wall and promptly kicked his ankle.

His stomach lurched with the realization that their escape plan was on display unless he could keep Sergio and Manuel distracted. Risking a look behind him to check out the damage, he spotted the narrow stream of water running from the corner of the window down the wall.

Suddenly, the two guards stopped their constant arguing, and the weight of their gazes landed heavily on Will's shoulders. He whipped around, calming the knot in his stomach.

"How are we supposed to empty these canisters?" he asked.

Sergio cocked his head as though trying to understand, but his forehead and lips wrinkled. Manuel didn't even pretend to try. Instead he sauntered toward them, pointing his chin at the materials littering the tabletop.

"Why is it taking so long?" he asked in Spanish. "When do you open up the Morsyni?"

Jess had caught the last word, and apparently guessed what was being asked. Letting out a sigh, she said, "Time. It takes time."

The guard frowned and slammed a palm on the counter, apparently understanding enough English to dislike her answer. "But there's two of you now."

Grumbling as she held up an outdated scale, Jess didn't bother to respond. Instead, she picked up a stoppered vial, walked over to the sink and poured something brown and chunky down the drain, wrinkling her nose as she did.

Sergio covered his own nose and grunted, and Will was tempted to do the same.

A sudden quiet descended as the driving winds and rain of the monsoon moved on, leaving only the wheezing of the air conditioner. Manuel looked at Sergio for a long moment before he announced, *"Vámanos."*

When the two guards stepped out of the lab, Will checked the back wall. The water trail had stopped growing, and would likely vanish by the time Manuel and Sergio returned. Will's shoulders relaxed. They'd been able to distract them this time, but they might not be so lucky the next.

He and Jess had to be on that transport.

Spicy rice and black beans from dinner rolled over and over in Jess's stomach as she leaned against the wall beside her door. Will had told her to eat as much as she could, because he didn't know when they'd have another chance. And then he'd reminded her to be ready as soon as the compound went to sleep. She had heard the telltale sounds of men moving toward their barracks nearly an hour before. Slamming doors, drunken shouts and rumbling voices had faded at least thirty minutes ago.

Still Will didn't show.

Jess pressed her fists into her eye sockets, swallowing down the bitterness that threatened to push her to the floor. She'd waited for him another time—the morning after she'd told him of Sal's proposal.

But Will said he was different now. He'd said she could count on him. That he'd get her out of here.

Clearly, her dad trusted him. After all, he'd handpicked this particular SEAL to send to her aid. So why wasn't Will where he said he'd be?

The lock popped and her door swung in, just enough for the shadow of a head and shoulders to appear around the corner. Will's eyes narrowed on her and he jerked his head toward the courtyard. "Let's go."

Suspicion fought with the urge to trust him, but whether she was ready to rely on him or not, she knew this was her best chance of survival. She forced herself to take a step and then another.

She trailed behind Will through the shadows and down an alley between her building and the snoring that drifted from the neighboring barracks. They crossed behind the big house, which had lights still on in one of the upstairs rooms. Will grabbed her hand and tugged. She was so close she could smell the soap he'd used on his hair.

Suddenly her foot disappeared into a puddle, and she grunted at the flood in her shoe.

Will didn't slow down, but peeked over his

shoulder and squeezed her hand. His nod seemed to ask if everything was all right, and she answered with a quick bob of her own head.

Shadows loomed before them as they dashed along the base of the security wall. When they reached the corner, they turned with it. Will never eased his pace, even as the silence pressed down on them.

Jess risked a glance up at one of the guard towers. "Do you think someone's in there tonight?"

"I'm sure of it."

Fear raced up her back until her scalp tingled. Despite the slickness of her hand, she held on to Will's, following his every step.

A crash of metal resounded from the nearest barrack, and Will slammed to a stop. She had to fall into the wall to keep from running into him. Rubbing her shoulder, she glanced around him, even as he pulled her closer.

A loud shout sounded and a beam of yellow light flared from a window not far in front of them.

"Stay close." His arm snaked around her waist, pulling her chin into his back as she nodded, and the sharp, tangy soap she'd smelled earlier enveloped her senses. He jogged toward the building still ringing with the early-morning commotion and ran along the wall. They dodged the square of yellow light on the ground, ducking below the window ledge.

"Are we still going to try to get on a truck?"

He responded with a curt nod as he stepped into the open alley between two buildings. "If we can make it to the lab and back in time."

Jess's arm was nearly jerked out of its socket before she realized he'd taken off running, his fingers clamped around her wrist. Lights blazed in every window they passed now, and loud voices called to one another. Under the ruckus, Jess heard the sound of heavy, purposeful footsteps marching ever closer.

At least twenty yards from the lab building, Will jerked her against a wall, her elbow scraping the rough cinder blocks. "What—"

In a second he had his hand over her mouth, pressing her into the wall so insistently she felt it might give under the pressure. Her chest was already painfully tight from the excitement and running, and his palm blocked any real air she might find. In the darkness she could just make out Will's wide eyes, just before the elongated shadow of a hefty, overweight man spilled between the buildings. A guard—one she hadn't seen before.

Will's heart thundered against her palm, which she'd flattened against his chest. Pressing a finger to his lips, he took a step toward their visitor.

Her breath caught, and she clamped her mouth closed, praying for silence.

"Raul!" The voice came from several yards behind the armed guard—another of Juan Carlos's lackeys on night patrol.

Jess pressed her back against the wall, trying to disappear into the night, but Will stood in front of her, far too exposed and vulnerable, with only the corner of a building for cover.

Raul's shadowy figure turned, waving off his pursuer, who had called out to him, and kept marching right toward Will.

FIVE

Will took a deep breath through his nose and let it out, willing his pulse to slow, trying to make every second last an hour. The lights from the barracks cast an eerie, yellow glow into the darkness he'd been counting on to hide their escape. No matter how tightly they clung to the wall, if anyone got close enough to spot them, he and Jess were sitting ducks.

Five yards away, Raul grunted and scratched his gut. His companion had turned around when Raul waved him off and ambled back toward the courtyard. Raul's lone shadow moved across the grass path as if he hadn't even realized Will and Jess were there.

Will wrinkled his nose as sweat peppered the back of his neck. They were just in the wrong place at the wrong time, and it spelled disaster.

And he had only two options.

Fight or run.

Will could easily take the guy, especially with

the element of surprise. But not without blowing his cover as a mild-mannered scientist. And certainly not without drawing plenty of attention.

Three yards from the corner, the guard must have seen a shadow, because he suddenly shifted his grip on his weapon. He held it tighter, his steps becoming slow and methodical. "Is someone there?"

Will reached for Jess's hand and squeezed it. Even in the dim light he could make out the tight line of her lips and the rapid blinking of her eyes.

No matter what happened, he couldn't risk leaving her to face these men alone, so his only option was to run.

He pulled her close and pressed his lips against her ear. "Let's go."

She blinked once, nodded and took off.

His shoes slipping on the wet grass, Will stayed on her six as they reached a corner.

"Turn." With a hand at her waist, he steered her into a passageway between more barracks, but a glance over his shoulder revealed that he'd been a fraction of a second too late.

"Is someone there? Stop! I see you!" Raul screamed after them, his incredible girth bouncing as he chased them. They had to find a hiding place. Now.

Raul's labored breathing was dropping farther behind, but it wouldn't take long for him to reach the alley. There was nowhere to hide. On either side there were only gray cinder block walls, leading straight toward the center of the courtyard.

Suddenly Jess slipped into a crevice he hadn't noticed. They raced between two walls, charging for the big house.

"Up here." Jess jumped onto one of the plastic trash bins behind the house, grabbed the eave of a small shed and pulled herself onto the roof. There wasn't time to appreciate her athletic moves as he followed, yanking his foot up just as Raul reached the crevice that they'd used. The heavy-set guard leaned against his thighs and panted as if he'd just finished a marathon rather than a fifty-yard dash.

Will and Jess squatted at the edge of the shingled roof—one of the few in the compound not made of tin—with a perfect view of the path they'd just taken.

Raul looked around the larger alleyway, spun twice and then pointed his weapon down the narrow path.

Another guard ran up to him and swore loudly. "What are you doing? Get back to the truck."

"But I think I saw someone."

The taller man made a slow circle and squinted in the direction that Jess had taken them. Her fingernails dug into Will's forearm as the new guard lingered, squinting toward the big house.

"You're seeing things," he finally mumbled. "Go back to work."

"I'm telling you, there's someone out there." The guard's voice dropped so low that Will couldn't make out another word, but the other man pushed Raul's shoulder.

"Don't be stupid. It's just the guys." He glanced around one more time. "Who else would be up at this time of night?"

Raul shrugged, but continued spinning in slow circles. "I don't know. But I know I saw something."

Raul's friend shook his head hard. "The boys are restless tonight. Jumpy. They know something's coming."

"What's coming?"

"Shut up and get back to work watching the trucks."

Raul's friend was clearly the leader of the two, and while Will could make out only his profile in the darkness, his posture suggested that he expected to be obeyed.

Finally, Raul nodded. *"Sí."* He lumbered away as his friend took one more look down each of the paths in the area. Clearly satisfied that Raul had imagined the whole thing, the second guard finally strolled toward the courtyard and disappeared beyond one of the trucks.

Jess's grip on Will's arm slowly relaxed, and she clasped her hands around her bent knees.

She glanced at him for a split second, as though she couldn't risk more than that. Maybe she thought if she looked away from the winding paths and alleys before them, she'd miss Raul or one of his friends returning to find them.

But they were alone for the moment, with no one for at least twenty yards in each direction. A balcony on the big house hung over their hiding spot, blocking the moonlight that poked around lazy clouds. The ruckus within the barracks had settled, lights going dark once again. Every few minutes good-natured yelling from the guards in the courtyard pierced the night, but other than that, all was silent and still.

They were safe. If just for a minute.

Will risked a quiet whisper. "Did you catch much of that?"

She only shook her head, her long braid flopping over her shoulder.

He quickly translated the gist of the conversation, and she nodded slowly, never quite meeting his gaze. "What's coming?"

"Juan Carlos."

Finally, Jess looked directly at Will and hugged her knees even tighter.

If he hadn't been so highly trained, he would have been doing the same thing. Juan Carlos's plan to attack a neighboring cartel had the whole compound off-kilter. And the two of them were in the middle of it.

"So how'd you know about this place?"

Her shoulders relaxed enough that he could actually differentiate them from her neck. "They've been making me stock the lab, and a lot of the stuff that we're unpacking was stored in this shed. I spent the first couple days here digging out beakers and hot plates and all the other ancient equipment I could find."

"And you remembered that it had a shingle roof and trash cans?"

She lifted a shoulder and shook her head. "I paid attention. I thought I was on my own here. I didn't know if anyone would find me."

The words settled, heavy and bitter, in his stomach. "And if I hadn't come?"

She glanced at the towering wall lined with barbed wire and broken glass. "I was going to crawl up here, jump the fence and face whatever was on the other side." Her voice wavered on the last word, a touch of uncertainty in an otherwise fearless statement. He had to cross his arms over his chest to keep from pulling her against him and kissing the top of her head, as he'd done a thousand times in their previous life.

Her escape plan would have been a suicide mission. No intel. No protection from the elements. And no training.

He'd been trained by the very best to survive under those conditions, and the thought of landing in the middle of an unknown jungle still twisted his gut.

On the lam from a drug cartel with zero ethics, her escape plan would have ended badly, and she knew it. But it wouldn't have stopped her from trying.

Her courage made Will smile. It was going to come in handy in the next week.

"I'm glad my dad sent someone." She rested her chin on her knees, and his gaze joined the motion of hers, sweeping across the winding paths between buildings.

Of course, she hadn't specified that she was glad it had been Will.

If he'd read her right, she had been surprised when he opened her door earlier that night, even though he'd told her he'd come. Her trust in him was hazy at best, but he couldn't fix that overnight. Ten years of questions and bitterness didn't disappear in two days.

"Me, too."

"Hmm?"

He nudged her shoulder with his own. "I'm glad that your dad sent me, too."

The corner of her mouth tugged upward in a

tiny smile that disappeared an instant later, when a low rumble sounded. She looked toward the balcony above, as though waiting for lightning to follow the thunder. "What is that?"

He nodded toward the hive of activity out in the courtyard. "Our getaway."

The trucks shook and rattled as their engines roared to life, drowning out the shouting of the guards and likely waking anyone within the compound.

"They're going without us, aren't they." She didn't ask it as a question, instead angling her head to indicate she knew it to be true. With a squeak and a groan, the front gates rolled open and the trucks lumbered through, disappearing into the blackness. "So what are we going to do?"

He clenched his jaw for a long moment. They couldn't count on more trucks arriving in the next few days. And even if one did show up, the way the two that just left had been guarded, he couldn't count on even getting near another one, either.

Taking a deep breath, Will scooted to the edge of the roof. "Everyone's distracted. Time to get back to our rooms."

He dropped to the ground, bending his knees to take the impact. Turning, he put his hands up to catch Jess around the waist, but she had already jumped onto the trash bins. With an easy hop and a sly smirk, she joined him on solid ground.

Fair enough. This wasn't the first time she'd proved that she didn't need him. And maybe she didn't. But she had him, anyway. At least until she was safely back in San Diego with her father watching over her. Preferably in plenty of time for Christmas. They had an escape to make and a lot of jungle to cover in just two weeks.

Will led her to the shadow of the security wall behind the house and slipped to the corner.

"No, really," she whispered. "What are we going to do?"

A glance around a corner showed that all was clear, and he bolted for the protection of the next building, hauling her behind him. "First, we're going to take advantage of any intel we can find."

"Like what? Memorizing the guard rotations?" Her words were still quiet, but marked by panting breaths.

"Yes. And getting our hands on a map of this jungle, if possible. We have to figure out exactly where we are, to get to where we need to be." He pulled her across another alley, always listening for the sound of footsteps.

"Where exactly are we going?"

"Panama City. If we can get to the U.S. Embassy, we can connect with the DEA and get home."

She nodded, rested her head against the wall, then shot up straight. "The DEA?"

"Yes. I told you about that." Her expression told him that she didn't remember, so he explained. "My friend who arranged for me to be invited here—" Jess snorted at this choice of words "—is DEA. She put a GPS tracker in my shoe. But it pings off of cell towers, and I have a feeling we're too far from the nearest tower for them to get more than a general location. Even if they do, they'll have to put together an official op to come for us. We can't count on that. Especially before Juan Carlos gets back."

Jess's eyes narrowed, creating a little wrinkle at the top of her nose. "Why didn't she put one of those high-tech satellite trackers on you?" The skepticism in her voice rang loud and clear.

"This isn't an official op, for the navy or the DEA." He tugged her away from the wall. "She couldn't afford to lose an expensive piece of equipment, and I couldn't risk having our hosts find that on me."

They fell silent as they wound their way back toward her room, but when they reached the door, she stopped just before sliding inside. "So after we gain all this intel, how are we going to get to Panama City?"

"We're going to use your plan."

"Mine?" Her dark eyebrows rose in twin arches.

He gave her a little push inside. Just before he closed the door, he said, "We're going over the wall."

Jess sucked air through her nose and let it out in a slow breath as she stared at the lab equipment in front of her without really seeing it. Even after a mostly sleepless night, and at least a couple hours contemplating Will's idea to jump the fence, she was no closer to seeing how it was possible.

"You okay?" His voice was right in her ear, and she jumped, nearly yanking the hot-plate cord off the machine. "You seem tense."

"Really? I can't imagine why." She shot him a sharp glare, but immediately regretted her sarcasm. "Sorry. Guess I'm just tired. Didn't sleep well after…well, you know."

"I do." Sparing a wink for her and a glance at Sergio, their lone lab guard for the day, Will dropped his voice even lower. "I was thinking last night, when I was outside your room—"

Despite the muggy afternoon, goose bumps exploded down her arms, and she abandoned all pretense of paying attention to the boiling water in front of her. "You didn't go back to your cell last night?"

"'Course not." He was so matter-of-fact about it that she wondered why his words had surprised her.

"Hey!" Sergio leaned against the wall, one knee bent and foot pressing flat to the cinder blocks at his back. He rattled something off in Spanish, waved his gun and returned to picking at a piece of breakfast still stuck between his teeth.

Jess didn't have to speak the language to know that he wanted them to pipe down and get back to work. But how was she supposed to concentrate on emptying the metal cans when all she could think about was Will's cryptic words the night before? He had to have a plan, because even she knew hers had been woefully inadequate to really get to safety. And he was the one trained for these kinds of situations. He was supposed to take charge and get them out of here.

Except…except it was easier to know that in her heart than it was to keep her doubts from surfacing with each of his promises.

By the time lunch rolled around, Sergio wasn't even pretending to watch them anymore. He yelled something, kicked the door open and then stepped into the midday sun. Without a look over his shoulder, he closed the door on them, and Jess, who hadn't been unguarded in the lab since she'd arrived, couldn't repress a low giggle. "I suppose he's as tired of watching us unpack musty boxes as we are of doing it," she said.

This earned her a half smile that quickly disappeared as Will hurried across the room and jumped onto the counter. "Will you watch the door? Sergio said he was hungry, so I guess he went to find some lunch. But he'll be back. Whistle as soon as the door starts to open."

"What are you doing?"

He pointed to the window that he'd opened the day before. It was barely as wide as his shoulders, which, to be fair, weren't as skinny as they had been in high school. "I'm collecting intel."

She rubbed her hands together and walked in his direction. Her thoughts weren't quite formed when she opened her mouth, the words tumbling out. "Maybe I should do that." She waved a finger in his general direction. "I mean, you have to squat to keep from being seen. I'm short enough that I could stand there easily."

He glanced down at his thighs, which were indeed straining to keep him at the right level, and shrugged. "Sure. If you want to."

"I do." Accepting his outstretched hand, she let him pull her onto the counter. Scooting in beside him, she gripped the edge of the sill with her fingertips and pulled herself up just enough to peer into the courtyard. The location of the lab gave her a partial view of the grassy common area and the big house, blocked by some of the neighboring buildings. "What should I be looking for?"

He let out a loud laugh, and his white teeth flashed in the grim room.

A battle raged within her—one side wanting to enjoy his laugh, which had always put her at ease and warmed her heart, and the other wanting to slug him for laughing at her. The latter won, and she pushed his shoulder with her fist.

Will's body swayed, which just brought on another chuckle. "What did I do?" His eyes twinkled as he bit his bottom lip—most likely to keep from laughing again.

"Oh, you know what you did, William Gumble."

"Now it's getting serious." The crinkled lines below his eyes implied just the opposite. "No one has double-named me since I turned twenty-five."

"Not even your grandmother? I seem to recall she was pretty fond of calling you by all three of your names once upon a time."

"Nope." Will took a little step forward, crowding Jess's personal space. "Abuelita passed away three years ago."

"Oh. Will." Jess's words were more sigh than anything else, and suddenly she was too far away from him. Close enough to feel the air around him stir as he sucked in a quick breath was still too far. She needed contact. She pressed a flat hand against his side.

He didn't jump or even acknowledge her touch until he turned slowly. Her hand stayed in place and by the time they were face-to-face, she was halfway hugging him. His brown eyes were clear, but sadness loomed in them and she could almost see him fight off the pain of his loss as he ground his teeth.

It was that visible battle to stay in control that made her throw her other arm around his waist and hold on for all she was worth. Pressing her ear against his chest, she counted three heavy heartbeats before he slipped his hands around her back, resting his chin on top of her head. His arms were solidly muscled, but their embrace was gentle. As she sank into his hug, her stomach twisted at the memories. How many times had they stood just like this, holding on to each other because everything else was flying apart?

"I'm sorry I wasn't there. I didn't know." She squeezed him just a little bit harder. "I would have been there for you and Sal. Even though…you know. I just— I would have been there."

"Thank you. I know you would have." His hand rested on the side of her head and callused fingers followed her ponytail from the rubber band to its tip, tugging gently on the end. Not wanting to move away from his warmth and the comfort of his arms, she snuggled in closer.

"I was deployed. Only three weeks shy of my R & R. I knew she'd been sick, but I thought I'd get a chance to say goodbye."

Jess tried to speak, only to be silenced by the

sorrow choking her. Abuelita, his grandmother, who had welcomed Jess to every Gumble family dinner and always told her to eat more—to put some meat on her skinny, fifteen-year-old bones. Jess couldn't believe she was actually gone. Or how well Will was handling it.

Of course, he'd had three years of ebb and flow to smooth the pain, like waves over a seashell.

But the news cut Jess like a dagger, acute and angry. And all too familiar. Moms and grandmothers left. It was just the way of the world.

The simmering agony just below her sternum reminded her that she'd dared to hope that Abuelita would be different. Jess had wished that if anyone could break the mold, it would have been the little woman—barely four foot eleven—with the shock of white hair and skin that glowed like burnished bronze. Surely that strong, stubborn woman had loved her family too much to ever leave them.

Will swiped his hand in a large circle over Jess's back, helping her return to the present. "She'd been fighting it for more than a year, and my mom said she'd been doing pretty well. But after the last round of chemo, I think she was just too tired to fight anymore." He swallowed thickly. "Last time I talked with her, she said she missed my granddad. I think she was ready to see him again."

That must have nearly killed Will. A man who didn't know how to quit had had to grieve for a woman who just couldn't keep fighting. A sob caught Jess off guard at the awful thought, and she hiccuped, essentially shattering the solemn moment.

Will jerked away, putting his hands on her biceps and looking right into her eyes, frowning at the tears he saw there. "I shouldn't have said anything."

"No. No. I'm glad you told me. I just… I'm just sorry I wasn't there." *For you.*

And for Sal, too.

The two brothers had been so much more than good friends. They'd been her stable family after her mother had decided she didn't want to be a mom any longer. After Jess had wound up with a deployed father and a forgetful great-aunt.

Sal had made Jess feel important and beautiful, as if her mixed-up family didn't define her. She'd adored him for that.

But Will had been special. Confident and so sure of himself. While Jess had been gangly and awkward, Will had always been precisely Will. And for six years he treated her as if she was the missing part of his family. He had too many cousins to name, and somehow his smile when she entered a room made her think he'd been lonely until she'd arrived.

Jess was lonely without Will, too.

It wasn't a teenage crush or hero worship. It was simply knowing that he understood her. Knew her.

But now she knew almost nothing about Will.

The corner of his mouth lifted into a crooked smile that didn't even begin to reach his eyes. "She loved you, you know. And she would have loved hearing this story."

"This story?" Jess said.

"Yep. About how you were kidnapped and I got myself kidnapped to find you." His smile began to swoop into a dimple in his right check, turning back the clock ten years. "And how we escaped. Together."

Knuckling away a tear that refused to be blinked into submission, Jess bit the corner of her mouth. "You really think we will?"

He shot a glance toward the window beside her. "If you quit crying and start looking for something useful."

She shoved at his shoulder, but chuckled as she rested her nose on the sill, four fingers clinging to it on either side of her head. Will jumped from the counter and moved silently across the room. In fact, she realized that he'd taken up a spot near the door only when the weight of his gaze on her back made her glance around the room.

Outside, nothing was out of the ordinary. Men

in pseudomilitary uniforms marched through the courtyard, which the monsoons had turned into two parts swimming pool, one part tar pit. Most of the buildings were abandoned at this time of day, while workers harvested or planted crops.

A man in khaki pants and a white cotton button-up carried a briefcase straight through the middle of the mire. The hems of his pant legs grew black as mud covered his shoes and then clung to the fabric. He ignored it all, just marching toward the big house and pushing up his sleeves with every third step.

Jess let her gaze sweep over the rest of the yard, watching for anything else of note.

If the guards at the front gate made a midday switch, they'd already done so, because they stood as still as the gargoyles carved on ancient cathedrals that she'd seen on her pregrad school trip to Europe.

But this place didn't remind her of any church she'd ever entered. And she was probably the only one calling out to God here. Even if she sometimes wondered if He was still listening.

An annoying voice in the back of her mind reminded her that Will had been an answer to her prayers, whether she accepted that fact or not.

She frowned at the guard tower at the corner beyond the big house, forcing her mind off Will and his presence. Except she could still feel his gaze on the back of her neck, as warm as his arms had been. Which had been kind of nice. And he'd smelled really good.

"Erg." Why couldn't she stop thinking about him?

"Did you say something?" Will sounded mildly amused, and she could picture the smirk on his face, complete with the return of that too-cute-for-a-SEAL dimple.

"No." She made another visual sweep, past the big house and the smaller building sitting just to the left, before something out of place yanked her gaze back.

The man in the white shirt and mud-caked khakis walked right past the front door of the main residence and opened the door of the neighboring building. Strange. Briefcases and suits usually came and went through the front entrance of the big house, but this man moved with assurance and opened the door, certain of his reception within.

For a fraction of a second, she could just make out the form of someone behind a desk sitting in the entryway. Another man pushed white papers in front of him before the new arrival slammed his briefcase down on top of the documents.

"Do you know what that building is?" she asked.

Will's hand pressed against her shoulder before she even realized that he'd moved. "Which one?"

She pointed. "Next to the main house. Just to the left."

As they stared at it, the door opened wider than it had been before. Mr. Pushy Sleeves stopped to look over his shoulder. His reflection twisted in the glass of a mounted picture on the wall behind him. Jess tried to catch a glimpse of the artwork hanging in the frame, but it was too far away.

Will's shoulders tensed as the man headed toward the front gate. "That was a map hanging there."

"Are you sure?"

"Not at all." He shook his head, never taking his gaze off the building in question.

Shrugging a shoulder, Jess went back to watching the yard. "So it means nothing."

"Not quite. If there's a map in there, then there might be other maps and useful intel, too. If it's an administration building, we might be able to find something that tells us what we'll be facing when we escape and exactly where we are."

She blinked hard. How had he gotten all that from one tiny glance into a building so far away?

Before she could spend more than a nanosecond on the question, the handle on the lab door jiggled. Her eyes flew wide, matching Will's.

Her heart hammered as she scrambled to crawl from their perch, knowing she would be too late.

The door creaked.

And suddenly Will grabbed her around the waist, hoisted her off the counter and set her on the floor without a sound except for her "eep" of surprise.

Her gaze jumped from the shockingly stable floor beneath her feet to Manuel's odd expression. His eyes narrowed, his features turning hard. His mouth formed some words that she couldn't hear through the roaring in her ears.

Will tapped her shoulder and her stomach lurched to her throat. She'd forgotten he was even there for a second, consumed as she was by the distrust written across Manuel's features.

Shoving her hands into the pockets of her apron, her fingers wrapped around the handle of a scoopula. She jerked it free and waved it in front of her face. Spinning halfway around, but never letting Manuel out of her sight, she said, "Here it is!" Her voice was too high and too sugary, so she gulped a shaking breath and tried again. "Let's get started."

To his credit Will didn't even raise his eyebrows. "Good. After you." Holding out a hand, he let her lead him toward the pile of supplies they'd unpacked so far.

Manuel's suspicious gaze following their every move made it clear he didn't believe that they'd really been looking for a simple tool, but he made no move to stop them. Jess pressed her shaking hands together before picking up two cans of tear gas.

"Time to try out the hood."

Will joined her, following her silent lead as she placed the metal cans inside the fume hood and sealed it up.

"Will you turn that on?"

Will pointed at a button, and she nodded. When he flipped the switch, the old vacuum coughed to life. She'd checked the filter on it when she'd first arrived, and hoped it was as clean as it looked.

After pushing her arms into the appropriate holes, she squeezed her eyes closed, held her breath and twisted off the lids.

Nothing happened.

Releasing her breath, she tipped one can over. It was empty. So was the other.

"These look like they've been used," Will said.

"Only one way to find out for sure."

After another fifteen minutes of them testing more equipment, Manuel finally relaxed against the wall. He let his gun dangle from the strap across his chest and then folded his arms over his stomach. His eyes drooped, and his breathing deepened until it wasn't possible to tell if he was actually awake or asleep standing up.

The hum of the hood and the scraping of metal against metal as they cleaned out the detonation pieces carried on through the afternoon, until

Will brushed her hair away from her ear and whispered directly into it.

"I'm going to find out what's in that building. Tonight."

When she opened her mouth, she knew that the sound about to emerge would draw Manuel's attention, which they couldn't afford. So she clamped her teeth together, biting the tip of her tongue and wincing at the searing pain.

Will seemed to take her pain as concern, quickly adding, "I'll be fine, and I'll let you know what I find."

She shook her head with so much force that her ponytail hit him in the side of the head. "Oh, you're not going in alone."

SIX

William pulled on Jess's arm just enough to angle her to face him. When he was sure he had her undivided attention, he shook his head very slowly and mouthed a single word. *No.*

There was no way on God's green earth that he was going to risk taking her on a reconnaissance mission. Two people meant double the chance of being seen, double the chance of losing his cover and double the chance of injury or even death.

Escape would work only if he flew under the radar until then. If either of them drew additional suspicion, they would draw extra guards. Getting out of this place was going to be hard enough as it was.

He wasn't going to back down on this.

Jess held his eye contact, shrugged and nodded. Her pink lips pursed into a determined circle that he'd seen on more than one occasion when her dad had told her she couldn't do something. She'd squint her eyes, make that face and promptly talk her dad into whatever it was she wanted to do. Usually that scenario involved some ill-advised road trip or midnight body surfing with Will and Sal. And always her argument had started with those pursed lips.

With a quick check on Manuel, who was still resting against the cinder blocks, she knocked over a tub of what looked like salt. A flick of her hand smoothed it out across the black surface, and she quickly spelled out her argument with her index finger.

I'm going.

Will jerked his chin from side to side. After swiping his hand to clear away her message, he wrote his own.

Not safe.

Her eyebrows pulled together as she wiped out his words. Her gaze fell to the salt chalkboard, her finger making even, sharp grooves in the crystals.

I can help.

What if you get caught?

She crossed her arms for a moment, staring at his question, and he let a little smile escape. He had her now.

Her hand cleared the board again, and as she slowly spelled out the words, he glanced up to make sure that Manuel hadn't woken up from his siesta. The guard snorted, his shoulders jumping, before his snoring settled back into an easy rhythm.

When Will looked back down, he nearly let out a snort of his own.

I won't if you're with me.

Jess's eyes shone as if she'd solved a complex scientific equation or figured out the world's oldest riddle. She thought she had him beat.

But that wasn't his biggest concern.

More than anything, he wanted to know why she was fighting him so hard in the first place. Why couldn't she just go along with his plan? Rescues. Escapes. Midnight missions. These were his job. And he was a pro.

But she just couldn't back down and let him take care of her.

He shook his head hard and gave up the silence of the salt. Maybe if she could hear the conviction in his voice, she wouldn't fight him so hard. Putting his hands on her elbows, he bent his knees until they were eye level. "It's dangerous."

Her head wagged back and forth and she opened her mouth, clearly ready to argue with him. After checking the volume of his voice, he cut her off. "Listen to me. If I'm caught where I shouldn't be, they'll try to kill me. But I can take care of myself."

"I'm not scared—"

He interrupted her without a pause. "I won't risk your safety."

She tapped the table with a frustrated staccato beat. It hadn't been particularly loud, but it must have caught Manuel's ears, as he popped up and swung his weapon around. Big brown eyes blinked fast in the fluorescent lights, and he rubbed a meaty hand down his cheek as his head lolled to the side.

Will dropped his hands and bit his tongue, his pulse in overdrive. Against his right arm, Jess's muscles tensed, too, her breathing shallow and her hazel eyes unblinking.

Manuel eyed them with distain. Apparently the cushy guard job wasn't any more fun for him than it was for them. He snorted again, making a sound in the back of his throat that would have gotten him kicked from Will's mother's dinner table. Swearing bitterly, he flung open the lab door and disappeared with a clang of metal.

Jess must have felt the same urgency to end their discussion that Will did. As soon as the handle clicked closed, she turned on him. "Do you actually think I'm safe here?"

"Of course not. That's why I'm here." He scrubbed his hand over his face, scratching at the whiskers on his chin. He was never this shaggy when he was stateside, and the beginnings of his usual deployment beard somehow only served to remind him that this op was anything but typical.

"Who knows what kind of information could be in that building?" She waved a hand in the general direction of his target. "You might need my help. And what if there's something in there that would let us escape immediately? Wouldn't you want to have me right there, so we can get out of here?"

If he'd been rescuing someone else—anyone else—he wouldn't have put up with any arguments. His job was to rescue. Her job was to be rescued.

But all this history behind them made him pause.

He could be the rescuer only if she allowed herself to be rescued by him. And right now, she just wanted to rescue herself...because she didn't trust him.

He couldn't blame her.

"You're right." A quick smile transformed her face, but he cut it off quickly. "We have no idea what's in that room. Or who's in that room. What are you going to do if there's a trap?"

Her grin melted into an expression of uncertainty, and he could see the wheels spinning behind her eyes.

"Listen, I can't let anything happen to you. I promised your dad." And Will had promised himself. He owed her at least that.

Some of the tension in her shoulders began to relax, the lines in her forehead easing as she slipped her soft hand into his. "I know. And I appreciate it. But I'm safer *with* you than anywhere else in this compound *without* you."

Tossing his head back, he glared at the buzzing lights and heaved a sigh.

She squeezed his hand just enough to get his attention. "You know I'm right." There was a smile laced into her words, and he didn't like it. At all. "Whatever's in that building will be easier to face together."

Swinging his gaze back to her face, he ignored the victorious gleam in her eyes. "If I let you come, you will do whatever I tell you. Without question."

She shrugged. "We'll see."

"No." His growl must have surprised her as much as it did him, because she yanked her hand out of his, pressing it over her mouth. He cleared his throat twice to level out his tone. "You'll do whatever I say without question, for your safety and mine. Or I'll leave you in your room tonight."

She didn't move for what felt like an eternity, but finally nodded. "All right."

When the door to her cell opened, as smoothly and as silently as ever, Jess slipped into the early-morning air, still thick with the prior day's rains.

Will's gaze traveled from the top of her head to her feet as though making sure that she hadn't been hurt in the previous six hours. She wondered what he saw when he looked at her.

Of course, she wasn't exactly at her best. She hadn't showered in three days and had been rotating two shirts for the past week. She was just glad she'd managed to wash her clothes once in her bathroom sink. Anything beyond that was gravy.

Whatever he saw, he didn't indicate. He just wrapped his hand around her wrist and nodded in the direction of their target.

They skirted the usual buildings, safe in the shadow of the perimeter wall as they drew close to the cartel's possible command center. Every window in the single-story building was black, and even the big house next door seemed especially quiet. Without the rumble and ruckus caused by the military trucks, the entire compound was eerily still. Raul and the guards from the night before were nowhere in sight.

Jess followed Will along the stucco wall. He paused at the corner, peering into the darkness, then turned and whispered over his shoulder. "Stay here while I find a way in."

"I'll go—"

He pressed his finger to her lips, gentle yet

insistent enough to stop the flow of her words. Heat burned her neck.

"Remember. No arguing tonight. I'll be right back."

She nodded, and he vanished. Jess sank against the wall as her heart hammered beneath her rib cage. With a timid pat she pressed two fingers to her lips, which still tingled, setting off a flurry in her stomach.

That was odd.

Will's touch hadn't ever set her nerves on edge before. In fact, no one had ever before sparked butterflies like those swooping and soaring in her now.

When her college roommates had whispered behind fluttering hands about their boyfriends, Jess had just assumed they were more excitable. But had she really been missing out on this sweet torture—the one that made the air thicker and the moon brighter—all these years?

So focused on school, she hadn't dated much after breaking up with Sal. Just Colby, another biology major, during her sophomore year in college. But even his kisses hadn't sparked her like Will's touch just had.

Of course, she and Colby didn't have years of history together. He didn't know about her mom's absence or her dad's deployments or Great-aunt Eva's burned dinners.

He'd never asked about them.

Then again, she'd never offered any of the details, either. And she'd wanted it that way. It was easier to keep him at a distance, to keep him from knowing her too well. Because people who said they loved her, left her.

After one semester, Colby had left, too.

But she'd never given him the power to hurt her.

Not like Will had.

Jess frowned and tried to wipe the memory of Will's touch away. But it wasn't as easy as she hoped. His presence seemed to linger, and she jerked away from the wall, her hands flapping as though she could shake off so many uninvited thoughts about her former best friend.

But they weren't easy to forget, especially with those pesky butterflies.

Where on earth had they come from? She didn't want them. She barely knew this Will. What she did know, she wasn't entirely sure she liked. He was bossy and stubborn. And always right.

She definitely was not attracted to Will Gumble.

Except the nervous flutters in her tummy didn't agree. Why couldn't they just get the message that Will was off-limits?

She'd been doing fine keeping up the wall between them. It was easier that way. As long as she didn't let him close, she didn't have to acknowledge that niggling voice that told her he was risking his life for her and she ought to forgive him.

At least she hadn't had to until he'd told her about Abuelita, and Jess literally couldn't keep from holding him.

Great. Now she'd think about that. Those arms made of steel. The gentleness of his embrace. The fact that he'd come back.

Just when she thought she'd go crazy if she had to spend one more minute dwelling on Will, the object of her errant imagination popped around the corner.

"I found an open window. Let's go."

Staring at the back of his slightly too long hair didn't do much to help her keep her focus on the task at hand, but a sudden squishing noise snapped her to attention. "What was that?"

He stopped and leaned his ear forward. "Let's just get inside."

They moved quickly and silently, but Jess couldn't shake the uneasy feeling that told her they weren't alone.

When they reached a partly open window, she didn't have time to do much more than brace her hands against the frame before Will caught her around the waist and boosted her up. In a flash she was through the window, somersaulting across a tile floor and into a solid wood desk with a terrible thump.

Her side connected with a desk leg, and she wheezed to catch her breath as Will crawled through the window and landed easily on both feet. He reached out to help her up.

"Thanks," she said, rubbing her side.

Will didn't respond to her mumble, but quickly made his way around the room. The darkness left her blind, but he seemed to have no trouble navigating the uncharted territory. He quietly called out what he found. "There's another desk over here, but it's clean." Wood thumped against wood. "And the drawers are locked. There's a rolling chair here, too. It's definitely an office of some kind."

When he found a door, he opened it, and his silhouette disappeared through the entrance. "It's a closet. Not too deep, but the shelves are stacked with boxes."

"What kind of boxes?"

"Like the ones you'd see at a law office. Records and stuff." Cardboard and paper shuffled, and she held her breath, hoping to hear more of what Will had found. "Just paper. Lots of paper in these boxes." He closed the closet behind him as he wandered toward another door. "Let's find the main entry. There weren't any windows in the front room with the map, so we can turn a light on."

She followed the sound of his voice, taking tentative steps across the room. When she reached him, he ran his hand down her arm until their fingers locked.

She reminded herself that it wasn't because he wanted to hold her hand, despite what her wildly firing nerves argued.

This was a safety thing. They couldn't stay together if they didn't hold on.

Will moved through the darkness as though he'd grown up in this building, while she ran her fingertips along the textured wallpaper just to ground herself in the space. Down the hall they reached a T, and without hesitation he hurried to the left. He passed one door, its wooden paneling darker than the wall, and then stopped at a matching one. Pressing his ear to the frame, he waited for a long second. With a click the door popped open, and they slipped inside, closing it behind them.

The room was impossibly dark, and Jess froze as Will dropped her hand.

Even the shape of his shoulders vanished into the blackness.

She'd never been afraid of the dark, but in that moment her breath caught. It wasn't the actual night so much as what it could be hiding that pulled her core muscles taut and dried her throat.

Suddenly, a light erupted in the far corner. At first she was blinded, and clasped her hands over her face, slowly separating her fingers to adjust to the filtered light. After several long seconds, she dropped her hands, blinked and slowly looked around the room.

A dusty brass desk lamp lit up a plain, unimpressive space. Large framed maps depicting the whole of Panama, mere decorations, covered pale brown walls. Grimy tomes lined floor-to-ceiling bookshelves on two walls. The floor was made of slabs of unfinished lumber. The single desk in the room was covered in heaps of papers, and Will was already there, shuffling through them.

"You going to help me or just stand guard?" Although his voice carried a note of teasing, the tilt of his head suggested that if she wanted to be useful, she had better get started.

At his side she sifted through piles of papers and ledger books that most likely tracked the cartel's illegal activities. Page after page of lists and numbers, and Spanish words scribbled in the margins. All of it was little more than gibberish to her.

"There's nothing here," she sighed.

Will glanced up at the wall, where a clock

ticked off the seconds, taunting their failure. "Keep looking. We've still got a few minutes."

Just a few minutes before they had to get back to their cells. A few minutes before someone might discover them missing. What could they possibly find in that time?

Jess jerked on a drawer handle, and it popped open. More red leather-bound ledger books were stacked nearly to the rim. Digging through them, she found a brown document sleeve. Pulling it free, she flipped open the cover. It was filled with oversize pages, and as she spread them across the desktop, she realized they were maps. Wavy black lines covered the white pages. And they made absolutely no sense at all.

She could feel Will's chin at her shoulder long before his palm pressed against her back. She sneaked a peek at him out of the corner of her eye. He was bent forward, staring intently at the new discovery.

"From the looks of this, we're not too far from Panama City." His statement was so confident that she looked back at the map, expecting to see a clear you-are-here sticker. No such luck. Not even one in Spanish. In fact, she couldn't spot anything that indicated their location.

"How do you know?"

He pointed at the bottom of the page, his finger

following an inconsequential line that intersected a wiggling blue one, which had to be a river.

"This section here is called the Darién Gap. It's mostly jungle, along the Colombian border." He tapped his finger at another point on the page. "There aren't any roads into the gap, so we can't be that far south."

"How do you know all that?"

A slow smile worked its way across his face. "This is what I do."

"What's that mean?"

His forehead wrinkled for a moment, and she could see his internal debate over how much to share play out across his face. "On our SEAL team, my buddy Zig is in charge of coms— communications. Luke is the medic. Rock does demolition. L.T. is a language expert. Everyone has a specialty."

"And you read maps?"

"Something like that. You didn't think I'd come down here without doing any recon, did you? I studied as much intel about this country as I could get my hands on in thirty-six hours."

Of course he had.

He was no longer the kid who skipped class and tried to tempt her to do the same. She had to get that fact to stick. She'd learned to fend for herself without Great-aunt Eva or the Gumbles or anyone else during the past ten years, and she wasn't the only one who had changed.

"I figured we'd be in the eastern section of the country, but I couldn't know for sure. This pretty much confirms it."

Jess nodded as if she was following his train of thought, but the truth was she'd been too busy doing chemistry extra credit through a good bit of geography class to know Panama's topography.

Whether he picked up on her hesitation or not, Will continued. "The Panama Canal breaks the country into two almost even sectors. Northwest—" he swiped his hand over a section off the map "—and southeast. And Panama City is right on the canal. When we get out of here, we'll only have to go about seventy to a hundred miles."

Her tongue felt as if it had doubled in size. "Through the jungle?"

He nodded. "Right now, that's the only option we've got unless the cavalry shows up."

"Right. Your friend at the DEA."

He nodded in agreement. Leaning back over the maps and shuffling them around, he said, "But we can't afford to wait for them."

The lines on the pages blurred, and she tried to follow Will's muttering, but it didn't make much more sense than the maps. Until he flipped a page to reveal a clear outline of the compound. The walls and guard towers were plainly marked, the big house dominating the back section in its grandiose style. The barracks, lab and even the mess hall looked like pop-up tents in comparison.

Around the outside of the security wall, someone had made more than three dozen red marks. They were spaced anywhere from one to three inches apart, almost like a checker board.

"What do they mean?" As soon as the question popped out of her mouth, she wished she could swallow it back down. She already had a pretty good guess, and if she'd escaped on her own, she would have had to face those red marks—whatever special brand of booby trap they might be—on her own.

"I don't know exactly, but you can bet they're a security feature."

After a few more pages of nothing significant, Will paused on the very last one. The map contained a single red circle and a winding red line leading to it.

Jess held the map closer to the light, squinting to make sense of the strange chart. "Look, is that us?" She pointed to the start of the red line, then at the circle at its end. "And another compound?"

"I'm betting they're not friendlies."

She shook her head. "Do you think this is the rival the Morsyni is intended for?"

"It's a solid—" He broke off abruptly at the same moment he pressed his finger to his pursed lips. His gaze settled just over her head, his shoulders squared and ready for a fight. "Hear that?" he whispered.

Closing her eyes and covering her own mouth with her hands, Jess listened, not daring to breathe. Spanish words in rapid succession slipped through the cracks at the front door.

Will's eyes flew wide. "They know someone's in here. Let's go. Now." He shoved the maps back into the folder, threw it into the drawer and flicked off the light before she could even make sense of his words.

Grabbing her arm, he towed her through the darkness into the hallway. She pulled the door closed behind her, and it clicked just as someone yelled.

Will's pace picked up. His feet were silent. Hers were like a buffalo.

And then another set of footfalls joined theirs, this one sounding like an entire stampede.

Her heart beat a painful tattoo in her throat.

The man chasing them was falling behind. But not fast enough.

Suddenly, she was swung into the room with the open window. With a little shove, Will pushed her toward the farthest desk. "Hide. Under there. Don't move until I come for you."

She did as he said, rolling the chair out, crawling into its space and pulling it back to hide her.

Through a small fissure in the wood, she saw Will's form disappear into the closet, just as the stampede arrived.

A narrow beam of light swept across the floor, matching the cajoling tone of their pursuer. Over and over he asked who was there.

Her pulse thumped in her ears, drowning out his words.

The flashlight tracked toward her hiding place, the beam glancing over the crevice. And holding there.

A sudden hiccup demanded release, and Jess clamped her hands over her mouth and fought the tears that streamed down her cheeks. She pressed against the confining walls, doing her best to disappear, but the light didn't move.

Lungs burning. Ears ringing. Heart pounding. She'd been caught.

And then the flashlight flicked away, toward the closet.

No. No. No. No.

The man's footsteps carried him toward Will's hiding spot.

Dear Lord, please don't let him find Will.

Her mouthed words didn't get very far as the old doorknob illuminated under the man's search.

Paralyzed, Jess could only watch and send an incoherent plea heavenward. If God was still around and had answered her prayer for a rescuer, He wouldn't take Will away so soon, would He?

Will had to be okay.

A disembodied hand appeared in the flashlight's beam.

Her heart stopped.

And their pursuer flung open the closet door.

SEVEN

Will closed his eyes, focusing on the sounds outside the closet instead of the twinge in his shoulders as his muscles tensed.

Their pursuer hadn't found Jess, and he was focused in on Will's hiding place.

Taking a deep but silent breath, Will shifted his foot against the wall, adjusting his leverage and easing the strain on his hamstrings.

He could sense rather than see the turn of the knob.

God, I'm ready, but if I don't have to fight, I don't want to.

Hinges squeaked. Feet shuffled. Light flashed directly below him.

Will didn't move, keeping his hands pressed against the front wall, his feet against the back. High above the door frame, he hovered, absolutely still.

The beam swept from side to side three times, and a mop of shaggy brown hair leaned into the narrow space, its owner surveying the shelves and empty floor.

"Where'd he go?" the man mumbled, backing away slowly. Then, with a loud curse, he raced out of the room and stomped down the hall, his footfalls growing quieter, his swearing louder.

For three aching minutes, Will didn't move, and he prayed that Jess wouldn't, either. She hadn't argued when he'd directed her toward the desk. Maybe she'd really follow orders this time.

Wood scraped against the floor, and the pitter-patter of tiptoeing feet drew near.

Then again, she'd never been cut out for the navy. Taking orders wasn't exactly her thing.

Walking his hands and feet down the walls, he met Jess at eye level just before dropping back to the floor.

"Where did you— I thought he was going to— How did you…?" Her questions ran together in a frantic rush as her hands reached for him. She didn't seem to care what she touched, one palm running over his shoulder and down his arm, the other pressing firmly against the cotton T-shirt covering his stomach.

He stopped her hands only by enveloping them in his own and pressing them over his thundering heart. He couldn't account for the accelerated speed. His pulse had been even and steady until she'd sneaked across the room.

Her tiny hands trembled in his grip, and he wrapped an arm around her waist, pulling her closer. Quivering breaths shook her lips, slowing with every rise and fall of her shoulders.

"I thought I was going to lose you," she confessed.

He brushed a silver track from her cheek and was surprised to find it damp. The Jess he remembered never let anyone see her cry. She wasn't cut out for this, and he had to get her back to her dad.

"It's okay. I climbed up there." Her eyes followed his gaze to the ceiling, then immediately returned to his face. "We're safe for now," he said. "But they know someone was here. They'll be looking for people out of place. We need to get back to our quarters."

"Right. Just… I need a second."

He nodded against the top of her head and tried to think of anything other than how natural it felt to hold her like this. His mind flashed back ten years to the night when she'd come to him, terrified of Sal's proposal. She'd been scared then, too. Maybe they'd both been too young to realize it at the time, but he could recognize it now. At eighteen she hadn't been ready to consider marriage. Especially not after her parents' union had crashed and burned so spectacularly.

Will should have just held her. Like this.

He shouldn't have run.

But even then he'd known that simply holding her might not be enough for him. And he'd had no right to anything more—not with the girl his brother loved.

In this moment, as her breathing returned to normal and the tension slowly ebbed from her, Will ran his fingers through her hair, which was softer than anything he'd ever touched before. But the face he saw was Sal's.

Sal, who had saved Will from his own stupid arrogance. Sal, who deserved a better brother. Sal, who was still in love with Jess.

After holding her like this, Will completely understood why ten years hadn't done much to change his brother's feelings. Jess had a magnetism that drew men without words. It was enough to pull Will almost four thousand miles.

She looked into his face, her cheek resting against his chest, and a little smile played on her lips. "Thank you."

He tried to swallow against his suddenly dry throat, but instead of croaking a response, he only nodded. Then he squeezed his arm a little tighter around her waist.

Even in the dim light he could see her chin quivering, and he heard her little gasp. Did she, too, realize that this new nearness had gone from comfort to something entirely different?

Without thought or plan, he leaned forward. Just an inch. Just a tiny bit closer to her very essence.

Her mouth opened with a small but silent "oh"—an invitation if ever there was one. Her hands had been pinned between them, and she pulled one free to slip it to the back of his neck, where her cool fingers splayed into his hair. Her touch was a lightning bolt, setting every one of his nerves on fire.

He couldn't pinpoint how long he'd wanted this, but it didn't matter. He felt as if he were an inch away from water after trekking through the Sahara.

And she was still Sal's.

He tilted his head at the last second, resting his lips against her forehead. Then with stilted, vigilant movements, he put an arm's length between them, one hand still cupping her elbow.

"We should go." He nodded toward the window, ignoring the confusion clearly written across her face. "I'll go first. Just follow right behind me. I'll catch you."

He'd catch her, all right. But who was going to catch his wayward thoughts, which demanded to know what that kiss would have felt like?

"That's my window."

Jess tried to narrow her focus to the glass pane

that Will indicated, although he never slowed their pace, weaving between buildings, always alert to their pursuers. Or maybe he was just avoiding looking at her? She certainly didn't hear or see any signs of a pursuer that would require Will to be quite so vigilant. She was almost certain they'd lost anyone who might be following them. She hadn't seen anyone since the man with the flashlight ran off. In fact, by the time Will had gone insane and nearly kissed her, she was pretty sure the man after them had left the building.

"How do you get through that thing? It doesn't look big enough for a rat."

He chuckled under his breath and picked up speed. "When it's the only way out, you figure out how to make it happen."

But the window was at least six feet off the ground. She tried to picture how he hefted himself up and through without landing on his head, but every scenario ended up with him lying in a heap on the ground.

As though he could hear her questions, he continued, "I use the bed for a boost and go through feetfirst. Just a little twist of my shoulders, and I can get through without any major injury."

That made sense. But he had the bed only on the inside. "And getting back into your cell?"

He shrugged a shoulder as he stopped to peer down an intersecting alley. "Slightly more dangerous." His grin said everything she needed to know. He could handle it.

Like he'd handled her a few minutes before?

Rats! Was she going to dwell on his almost-kiss all night long?

Probably.

But that didn't mean she couldn't fight it. Sure, in the moment it had seemed like a great idea. With his arms about her, she'd never felt safer. The thudding of his heart had made her own amp up to match it. And those stupid butterflies she'd felt after he touched his finger to her lips had returned in spectacular fashion.

But she didn't have to think about it.

Especially since nothing really happened. He'd obviously changed his mind—or decided he'd never been interested in the first place—and she'd settled for the forehead kiss.

Pausing at another intersection, only about ten yards from her door, Will ran his fingers through his hair as he glanced over his shoulder. "You okay?"

"Sure." But not if the sight of his fingers combing his velvet-soft hair insisted on reminding her of the time she'd had her own fingers tangled in those strands.

"You're kind of quiet."

With a deliberate drop in her voice, she said, "I thought we were being covert."

That earned her another low chuckle and a little tug to make it the last few feet. "You're so smart."

"Top of my class at UCLA."

The lines under his eyes crinkled. "I guess you did better when you didn't have someone begging you to skip class every day."

"Something like that."

Except it really was nothing like that. It was more like after her dad deployed again, Will left and she broke up with Sal, she'd needed something to focus on. And school had seemed like the best option. Science required her undivided attention, so it had been a natural major.

By the time she'd realized how much she actually enjoyed it, she'd been halfway to her bachelor's degree. From there the postgraduate work had been an easy decision. It kept her memories of Sal's broken heart, Will's disappearance and her mom at bay.

Her studies couldn't quite make her forget her mom's disappearance, but in the thick of an experiment, Jess thought less about the letter she'd found lying on the kitchen table when she was twelve. It had been in a nondescript, white envelope, just a single page in her mother's sweeping cursive.

Jess's hands had shaken as she'd read the words through watery eyes. Lynn McCoy was tired. Tired of being a single mom when her husband deployed for months at a time. Tired of being a commander's wife—required to go where the navy sent them. Tired of always being the responsible one, while her husband went gallivanting around the globe.

The letter said she'd found a job back East, near her childhood home and that Sean and Jess should keep going without her.

In the following weeks Jess's dad had called everyone he knew trying to track Lynn down, and in the end Lynn had called the house, just once, to tell Sean to stop calling. She was fine, but she'd had it with her old life.

Jess heard the truth, plain and simple. Lynn didn't love her daughter any longer.

Ignoring all that pain and those terrible memories had made them bearable.

But there was no ignoring the man checking out her room to make sure it was safe for her to be locked in again. The man who had almost kissed her.

Stop thinking about that, Jess!

Will made a sweeping gesture, inviting her in. "Safe. Ish."

Jess managed a half grin, never making eye contact. "Thanks for checking."

"Try to get some sleep." She must have looked doubtful because he hurried to assure her. "I'll be right outside for the rest of the night."

"No." Her tone hit a high note that was much louder than she'd intended. "You have to go back to your room. If they go to check and find you gone, they'll know it was you in the office."

"There was no one near my building when we went past, and no one has sounded any alarm. I'm okay. I'll be careful, but I won't leave you and your wrench to fend for yourselves." He gave her shoulder an awkward pat—one that screamed so many words left unspoken.

Ready to argue again, she was cut short by a flicker in his eye.

"Listen to me, Jess. I know I haven't always come through for you, but right now, right here, I'm not going to let you down." *You can trust me.*

The silent words rang so loudly she was surprised that guards didn't descend on them right then.

Could she really trust him? To evade detection? To keep her safe? To get them both home by the holidays?

She couldn't answer all those questions right that minute, but the angle of his head seemed to request a response. Rubbing her hands together, she squared her shoulders.

"All right. But be careful."

"Always am." With a shrug and a wave, he closed the door, his footsteps immediately fading into the otherwise silent morning.

The wall snagged her black T-shirt as she leaned into it, covering her face with both hands. Her breath was warm against her dirty palms, her skin already sticky from sweat and humidity.

Between hiding under that desk and returning to this room, Jess felt as if her life had been upended. And she couldn't even pinpoint what had caused it.

It wasn't the kiss—almost kiss—or the terror of thinking Will had been caught. It wasn't the trembling in her stomach or the rush his gaze sent sweeping down her spine.

A man other than her father had asked her to trust him.

And for the first time in ten years, she actually wanted to. She just didn't know if she could.

Especially since that man was Will Gumble.

Will waited until the last possible minute to signal Jess that he was sneaking back to his room. When light flickered through the windows over his head, it was time to move on. Pushing his tired legs from their crouched position, he knocked on her window and took off running, winding past all-too-familiar cinder block walls.

When he reached his window, he grabbed the bottom ledge and pulled himself up, twisting his neck and shoulders to get first his head, then his shoulders inside. Bending at the waist, he reached for the floor. In one practiced motion, he lifted his legs and slid in.

He caught himself in a handstand that wouldn't win him any gymnastics gold medals, but certainly did the job. Injury free, he fell into bed, the squeaking springs a welcome sound to his weary body and mind.

Just thirty minutes. That's all he needed to recuperate, to recharge his batteries, to face another day in which he knew not much more than he had the morning before.

They were east of the canal. The other compound—probably another cartel—was just a few miles away. And booby traps outside the perimeter wall meant trouble. It wasn't much, but it sure spelled disaster if they did make it beyond the fence.

And disaster for anyone trying to get in.

Any drug lord in this area wasn't typically worried about keeping people inside the walls. Will and Jess were exceptions. Typically, those inside were loyal to the leader.

So all those red marks around the complex most likely weren't for keeping people in. They were for keeping people out.

This compound had been under attack.

And it didn't take a bioengineer to figure out that Jess had been brought here to retaliate.

It would be much too easy to spend the entire

morning playing out what the rest of the information might mean, but Will needed sleep more than he needed to put puzzle pieces together. He couldn't afford to let his senses get sloppy.

Rolling onto his side, he used his hands as a pillow and closed his eyes. He'd been asleep for about twelve minutes when the metal door of his room scraped against the cement floor.

Instantly alert, Will didn't move more than his eyelids to take in the sight of the two men standing in shadow in the doorway. He could make out only their shapes against the shockingly bright light of the internal hallway at their back.

The stockier man swore in Spanish, his voice vaguely familiar.

The other one held out his hand. "Pay up."

"I'm telling you, he wasn't here." The first guy shook his head violently as he slammed the metal door back into place.

As soon as it was closed, Will leaped from the mattress, flying across the narrow room. Pressing an ear to the wall next to the door hinges, he stayed absolutely silent.

"You've just been drinking too much. Give me my money."

"He wasn't there. I saw that bed empty!" The stout man's growl surely woke up anyone else sleeping in the three other rooms off the hallway. "It wasn't a fair bet."

"Why not? Because you lost?" Something heavy bumped into the other side of the wall at Will's shoulder. "You owe me twenty dollars, Raul. Today."

Will's ears twitched. Raul had been after them before. He had an eye, if not the speed, for chasing them down.

"I don't have it."

"What do you mean? It was your bet. Your idea." Will could hear the anger filling the slighted man's voice.

"Well, he wasn't there."

"You keep saying that, but he's there now, so I want my money."

"But then where'd he go?"

"Maybe he fell off his bed."

Will glanced around the empty room. Other than the rusted, metal frame holding up a sagging mattress, and a chipped, yellowish sink in the far corner, there was no cover.

The second man's voice dropped to a lethal whisper. "If he wasn't in there, then where was he?"

Silence. Far too much silence.

Pinching his fingers at the bridge of his nose, Will prayed that they'd forget about it and just let it go. That they'd chalk it up to one man's drunken hallucinations.

"I d-don't know." Raul's voice was weak and carried a little stutter.

The man who wanted his money cackled. "Then maybe we should find out."

"Shouldn't we tell Juan Carlos or El Jefe?"

"Tell them what? That you were drunk on guard duty? That you had to come get me to sound the alarm because you didn't want anyone to find you this wasted? Maybe we should watch the Americans first. Maybe they're up to something. It could be worth much more than your twenty dollars."

Will's stomach twisted into a painful knot, his palms suddenly slick as he wiped them down his dirty gray pants.

He was going to have to find a way out of this compound while being watched like a hawk by someone he couldn't identify.

EIGHT

Jess held out her plate, careful not to let a speck of food fall to the mess hall floor. After a night of restless sleep, she needed any energy the spicy calories could provide.

The cook glared at her, clearly recalling her spilled breakfast the day before yesterday. Ducking her head, she pulled her plate close and spun to sit down at the end of a long bench. Its sharp edges cut into the back of her legs, helping to keep her groggy mind alert.

She shoveled in two bites of the slop on her plate, swallowing before the texture could compel her to stop eating. Just as she lifted the third forkful to her mouth, Will plopped down across the table.

His eyes were rimmed in red and more bloodshot than she remembered them being the day before.

She glanced at Sergio and Manuel, who stood about ten feet away, their backs to their charges.

Other than the two guards and the cook, she and Will were alone in the room, most of the men having eaten and left for the fields long before.

You okay? She mouthed the words.

He surveyed the nearly empty room, then leaned forward. "We have a little problem."

Her stomach lurched, the mush in her mouth turning into a painful lump. She tried to swallow it, but her throat had closed.

Father in heaven, what if we don't make it home?

For the first time since Will's arrival, she acknowledged her fear and that very real possibility. She'd counted on making it home in time for Christmas. She'd planned on giving her dad the deep-sea fishing pole she'd purchased three months before. Since Will's arrival, she'd even allowed herself to wonder if she and Will could restore a hint of the friendship they'd once shared in San Diego.

But what if they didn't make it home at all?

What if this was the end of the line for them both?

She choked down her breakfast, cringing as it traveled down her throat and settled heavily in the pit of her stomach. Setting her fork next to her plate, she bent closer and kept her voice low. "What is it?"

A shake of his head sent the little lock of hair over his forehead dancing. "Not here."

Jess couldn't eat another bite, her stomach in complete mutiny, so she bit her lips together, pressed her hands into her lap and bowed her head.

The riot in her mind wouldn't let her form a coherent prayer. She just repeated the same mantra over and over. *You're alone. You're alone. You're all alone.*

First her mom. Then Will.

Had God given up on her also?

Manuel grabbed her arm and pushed her toward the exit. She went without a struggle or even a thought. In the yard she stumbled around a puddle, only to step all the way into another. Her foot disappeared up to her ankle in the muck, and she screeched. Will reached for her elbow, his sure grip keeping her from falling into the crater.

Inside the lab her steadiness didn't improve. Every time she glanced at Will, her mind flew to all the possible things that could have gone wrong in the two or three hours that she'd lain awake on her cot. If he'd been caught by a guard before making it back into his room, then he wouldn't be here with her. Would he?

Manuel scowled at her, his posture more tense than it had been the day before. His fingers pressed against his gun so hard they turned white, and his lip curled in an agitated sneer. His eyes slicing through her, he barked a word that obviously meant she should hurry.

There was an extra edge to his bark this morning. Usually he displayed his displeasure with unhappy grunts and squinted eyes, but there was a hatred there that she'd never seen before. Was it tied to Will's trouble? Or was it caused by something as innocuous as the terrible breakfast?

Her pulse thudded painfully at her neck and wrists, but she didn't look away from her guard as she massaged her gloved hands over the throbbing points. Then she dropped several canisters into sudsy water. As it splashed near the rim of the sink, Will sidled up next to her and took the scrub brush from her hand.

"Let me do that." His tone implied that he was asking for her permission, but the intention in his movements couldn't be denied. "How many do you need?"

"Six."

Focused on watching Manuel for any reason behind his bad mood, she didn't check to see if Will had complied or where he set the cleaned equipment. When she finally swung in his direction, her elbow bumped into a glass beaker filled with baking powder that she'd left sitting on the counter. As it flew through the air, time seemed to stand still. Jess windmilled her arms, reaching for it, but it shattered against the cement floor with a scream like a banshee.

Or maybe the scream had come from her.

Glass flew in every direction, bouncing off the floor, the cabinets and her apron, even as she scrambled back into Will, who hugged her waist and pulled her against his chest.

"Did you hurt yourself?" His breath played with the hair at the back of her neck that had pulled free of her ponytail.

She shook her head, trying desperately to tune out the bellowing from Manuel and Sergio. Lurching from the room, the two guards escaped, slamming the door behind them.

Will squeezed Jess briefly. "What was in there?"

"It's harmless. Mostly just baking powder."

He sighed, letting his arm drop from the embrace, and she leaned against the counter for a moment to catch her breath. After pulling over a metal trash can, he stooped to pick up the biggest pieces of glass.

Pulling paper towels off a nearby rack, she joined him, wiping up the white mess, careful not to tear her only pair of gloves on tiny shards.

"So, are you going to tell me what you meant this morning? What kind of a problem do we have?"

He tossed in two more hunks of glass before

answering. "Someone saw that I wasn't in my bed last night."

Her hands stopped moving, and she blinked at him.

"Just after I got back into my room, two men came in. They were arguing over a bet they'd made, about if I was actually in there or not. One of them—our friend from the other night, Raul—swore I hadn't been there earlier." Will kept his voice low, his gaze settling somewhere beyond Jess's shoulder. "The second guy didn't believe that I'd really been gone, but Raul was so adamant that he seemed willing to consider the idea in the end."

Her stomach felt as if she'd been surfing in a hurricane.

"But that's not the problem."

That didn't help. How could it get worse?

"Instead of turning us in, they're going to be watching me—us—to see what we're up to. I got the feeling that they think they can gain some information to leverage a promotion within the cartel."

A band around Jess's chest tightened until her breathing was ragged at best. "So some guys are going to be watching us more closely than usual. But you didn't see who they were? You can't identify them?"

"They were just in shadows." Will brushed at

a stain on his pant leg as if removing it was key to getting them out of the compound. "I only saw their outlines for a second before they went back into the hallway, and I only got Raul's name. And unless he's the only overweight guard they have here, I doubt I could pick him out of a crowd."

Even when he'd chased them onto the shed roof, it had been dark. Jess couldn't identify more than his round belly and nasally voice, either.

"Is there any chance that Manuel was one of the men?" The memory of his angry leer made her skin crawl, and she gave an involuntary shudder.

"No." Will stood and picked up the broom that had been tucked between the counter and the wall in the far corner. Sweeping up the last of the spill with slow strokes, he frowned thoughtfully. "I'd have recognized Manuel or Sergio's shape or voice. It wasn't either of them."

She held a dustpan for him, then rose to dump the contents into the can. Her knees popped as she stood, and she bent to rub them after squatting so long. "What are we going to do?"

"The only thing we can. Stick together and keep our eyes and ears open."

The rest of the day passed in a haze, Jess working on autopilot while Will watched her, concern crinkling the corners of his eyes.

She was nearly ready to begin cleaning up the workstation for the night, when someone barged into the lab. Manuel and Sergio jumped to attention, their slouched positions forgotten in the presence of the new arrival. Sergio managed a sloppy salute. "El Jefe."

El Jefe said something that put both guards at ease, but his obsidian eyes never left Jess. "*Hola. My apologies. I have not been in to check on you in several days." The little man bobbed his head in a mock bow, but his face never lost the stern expression. His mustache twitched, reminding her of her unhappy high school principal. Although high-pitched, El Jefe's English was actually very clear, and she couldn't help but wonder where he had learned it.

After years of Great-aunt Eva drilling formal etiquette into her, Jess had to bite her tongue to keep from greeting him in return. Her hands shook at the effort it took not to respond, and maybe even more so at the evil that flickered in his eyes. Will's attempt to comfort her by running the back of his knuckles down her wrist, just out of sight of their visitor, did nothing to ease her nerves.

But at least he was right by her side.

After a long standoff, El Jefe pasted a fake smile into place and turned to Will. "I hope you're settling in well."

"Tolerably." Will's response earned a low chuckle that didn't fit such a tiny person.

"Good. Good. And you have everything you need."

He hadn't really asked a question, but Jess answered, anyway. "Not even close."

El Jefe's head jerked in her direction. The change in his features was minor, but deadly intense. "Oh, really?"

She could manage only a nod as her fingers fluttered for Will's just below the edge of the table, latching on as soon as they found his. Jess attempted to pull from Will's strength, trying to keep her knees from buckling.

"And I suppose that's why you've been so slow to produce a demonstration."

She swallowed against the desert in her throat, but couldn't produce any real reply other than a hesitant nod.

"Or maybe you've been distracted." The drug lord gestured toward Will, but didn't break eye contact with her. "Yes, I think that's it."

She shook her head. "No. I need the help. I can't pressurize the canisters alone." She hated the way her voice jumped half an octave at the end, her lie clearly audible to her own ears. Or was it desperation she heard? She couldn't let this strange little man separate them. That's what Will had said. They needed to stay together or they'd never get out alive.

Finally, El Jefe looked away, his gaze settling on a squirming Manuel. Her only clue to the meaning in his rapid-fire Spanish was the gentle squeeze of Will's hand. It couldn't be good if Will was trying to comfort her.

"Manuel will take Mr. Darrow back to his room. He can stay there until you show us the poison in action."

Will pressed his shoulders back but other than that remained still.

Why wasn't he reacting? How could he be so calm, when her insides were threatening to fly apart at any minute?

Still he said nothing, so with a silent prayer for all the right words, she opened her mouth and let whatever was in there spill out.

"I need his help. But I'm not unleashing Morsyni just for a test run. It'll kill you, me and everyone else inside these walls." El Jefe wasn't impressed, crossing his arms over his round chest. "But if we work together—" she tipped her head toward Will "—we can show you how it will work."

"When?"

"Tomorrow." What a terrible thing to promise. What had she been thinking? Clearly, she wasn't. She was just going on instinct, and hers had never been very good. But Will leaned in closer, his presence familiar and reassuring.

El Jefe narrowed his eyes, said something else to his guards and then nodded. "Tomorrow at noon. You will show us. Everything."

"Yes."

He nodded again, then turned and marched out of the lab, slamming the door behind him.

Manuel and Sergio looked as shell-shocked as she felt, her knees buckling until she had to lean against the counter just to stay upright. Only Will appeared unaffected. Or was he? His jaw worked back and forth in a slow rhythm that drew her notice to the tension in his muscles.

He was angry.

Had she said the wrong thing? Said something that would hamper their escape?

Stomach rolling and eyes burning, she risked another glance in his direction. He didn't have even a half smile for her, but he leaned his hip on the counter next to her, turning more than a shoulder on the other two men.

After several seconds, during which she thought her lungs might explode, he spoke. "You did good, kid."

The burning behind her eyes turned into full-blown tears leaking down her face. Those words had been the highest praise they'd shared in high school. When she'd aced an exam. When he'd won the race. *You did good, kid.* It meant he thought she'd done a great job. It meant he was proud of her. It was everything their teenage selves just couldn't find the words to express.

And right now, it meant more than all the other accolades in the world.

Later, when they were alone, she was going to hug him for that. Just for knowing exactly what to say to make her heart smile, even when fear threatened to tear her to shreds.

"We'll work it out in the morning." Her words weren't as strong as she'd hoped they might be, but she was proud that she'd managed to get anything at all around the lump in her throat.

The sun had set long before, and Will had been at his post outside Jess's room for more than two hours. Leaning against the outside wall, which was slick with moss and mud, he imagined he could hear the deep breathing of her sleep.

He couldn't count the number of times she'd fallen asleep when they were watching movies late into the night. She had the cutest little snore. More of a snort, really. Just as she was dozing off, her nose would let out a tiny gasp, and then she'd be out, completely oblivious to the rest of the world.

He couldn't imagine that had changed over the years.

But her nerve sure had.

His chest swelled at the memory of her facing down El Jefe. She hadn't broken a sweat or looked to him for help. She'd just done whatever it took to keep them from being separated.

Will would have blown up the entire compound before he'd let that slick little jerk order him away from Jess. And he'd been just about to do something drastic—although he wasn't sure what—when she'd piped up.

She was something else, and he couldn't deny the pleasure he found in getting to know her all over again—even under these conditions.

This night was less muggy than the past three, and he took a deep breath, letting it soothe the tension in his shoulders. Closing his eyes, he listened to the sounds of the compound. Grunts from the neighboring barracks. A slamming door. Cicadas singing their night song.

And a hard thud followed by a painful grunt.

Will was at attention in an instant. Jogging to the corner of the block wall, he peered around the edge. With five other buildings close by, the entrance to Jess's room wasn't well lit. That had been a good thing.

Until now.

Every shape and shadow caught his attention, but nothing appeared out of place.

He closed his eyes to shut out all other distractions, honing in on the same voice that had grunted before. It was cursing now, all the words slurring together. "She thinks she's too good for us, does she? I'll show her." A figure staggered into the alley about twenty feet away. Even at that distance, Will could smell the odor of alcohol, heavy as if the man had showered in it.

Will's stomach clenched, but he let out a slow breath to keep his physical reaction in check. He had to control himself.

Maybe the drunk would pass out and Will wouldn't have to do more than watch him sleep it off.

More likely his drunk buddies weren't too far behind.

Will couldn't afford to be caught dispatching a threat to Jess—not that he'd have much trouble fighting off the louts he'd seen around the compound. But he couldn't risk being separated from her.

So he took another deep breath, promptly choking on the stench of the approaching man.

The visitor stumbled again, catching himself on the wall just ten feet from Jess's door.

Will squeezed his hands into fists, scraping his knuckles against the rough wall between them. The pain kept him grounded, kept his mind on the immediate, so he pressed into it.

With three more uneasy steps, the thug drew

even with the door to Jess's room. The wood creaked as he leaned a shoulder against it, his breathing labored by the short walk.

Will's own breathing had slowed to an even, smooth tempo as he played out what was going to happen. He had to let the drunk get into Jess's room, out of sight, before taking the man down or he risked a ruckus that was guaranteed to draw unwanted attention. While his training meant Will knew how to deal with the threat silently, he couldn't do anything to keep them from being seen if the guy's friends were around.

But the thought of Jess waking up to a strange man in her room was enough to make Will's stomach revolt.

He hated that she'd be terrified, and he knew that she would be.

Lord, please let Jess have that wrench handy.

He'd give anything to be able to rush into her room at that moment and defend her. To be the one who could save her from the terror ahead. To be her hero.

He'd wanted to be that man ten years ago, too.

The truth knocked him back against the wall. Covering his face with his hands, he gulped for air that suddenly felt scarce.

He'd never let himself analyze why he'd taken off after she'd shown him the ring Sal had given her. He'd told himself it was because he'd needed a change. He'd wanted to see the world.

But in this moment, he knew the truth. As he waited to save Jess, he saw his actions for exactly what they were.

Cowardice.

He'd run from everything that had terrified him—the very thought of loving Jess, and the sure knowledge that he was going to lose her to the brother he loved, the brother he owed more than money could repay.

What a fool he'd been.

Some would argue he still was.

Will blinked as he heard the door to Jess's room open, followed by two heavy footfalls.

On a hope and a prayer, he sprinted around the corner.

Before he even reached the door, a solid thump echoed from inside the room, and his heart stopped beating.

NINE

The weight of the wrench in her hand was too much, so Jess dropped it to the floor. She could barely hear the clatter for the ringing in her ears. Her entire body shook as she stared at the man sprawled on the floor. He was tall and lean, and smelled like a distillery explosion.

And he wasn't moving. At all.

Oh, God. Please say I didn't kill him.

But she couldn't get her arms and legs to move in order to check for his pulse.

She'd hit him in the head with all she was worth, but now what?

Her legs shook so badly that she couldn't keep herself upright any longer. She would have hit the floor if a strong arm hadn't slid around her waist and pulled her against a wall of solid muscle.

Although her instinct to fight kicked in, she didn't have the strength to do more than push at the hand on her hip. She couldn't even muster a scream.

"Hey. It's me. You're okay."

Will.

She sank against him, wedging her head beneath his chin and trying to soak up every ounce of his strength. His other arm twined around her waist, and she let him hold most of her weight, her legs still refusing to do their job. His shoulders lifted and fell in a steady rhythm, each exhalation fluttering her hair.

But her hands still trembled. The feeling of the wrench had been branded against every finger as it connected with the intruder's skull.

Will rubbed her back, the heat of his palm slowly easing the tension there.

"Shhh."

It wasn't until he said something that she realized she'd been babbling. Incoherent gibberish at best. But in her mind, she heard the accusations as if they rang through a bullhorn.

You killed him. You killed him. You killed him.

"It's all right." Will's hand moved from her back to her arm, soothing from shoulder to elbow. "Everything's okay."

But it wasn't. Nothing was okay. She'd heard the crack as the wrench had landed. She'd watched the intruder fall to his knees, crashing against the unforgiving floor. He hadn't moved since.

Even though she'd had no other choice but to defend herself, she'd killed him.

And she would have to live with that.

Will leaned away and looked into her face, his thumb brushing at the moisture pooling below her eyes. "I'm so sorry that you were scared. But he can't hurt you now."

A sudden sob caught her off guard and seemed to open the floodgates. "I—I think I k-killed him. He hasn't moved since I hit him."

Will's grim expression broke with a hint of a smile. "You didn't kill him."

"Yes, I did." Panic laced her words, and she wrapped her arms around her stomach to keep herself from flying apart, since Will wasn't doing the job anymore.

He caught her eye and shook his head with deliberation. "He's still alive."

Was he right?

Peeking behind her, she looked at the prone form. With the toe of his shoe, Will gave the man's leg a little shove. The intruder let out a groan as sweet as any sound she'd ever heard, and Jess let her chin fall all the way forward, weakness again overcoming her.

Fear and relief apparently both sapped all her strength and threatened to send her toppling to the floor.

"Feel better?" Will's voice held a hint of teasing, his eyes glinting in the sliver of moonlight coming through the open door.

She wanted to slug him in the arm, but mostly she wanted him to hold her again, to hang on to her until she didn't fear anything else.

Whether he could read her thoughts on her face or he wanted the same thing, he pulled her back into the circle of his arms.

"I thought I was going to have to…" Her hands slid over the taut muscles at his waist until they met in the back. "I thought I'd have to live with it. With the knowledge that I'd killed someone."

"I know. It's a hard thing to carry through life." His words rang with a pure knowledge of the truth. Will knew what he was talking about, given his career choice. "But you don't have to carry anything from this. You didn't do anything wrong. You were great." He gave a little chuckle as he smoothed her hair. "In fact, I think I'll talk to the CO about adding wrenches to our weapons inventory."

That made her laugh, too. And the humor helped release much of the tension that had been building in her neck and shoulders. In its place she felt a strange sense of uncertainty—a tugging in two directions.

She wanted to stay this close to Will forever, listening to the murmur of his heart and the tempo of his breathing. It was familiar and everything she'd dreamed it could be.

But equally as strong were the memories of

him disappearing. The unanswered calls and messages. The pages of emails that were never replied to. She'd driven by his house eight times before getting up the nerve to knock on the door, terrified that Sal would answer and she'd have to face him again.

Telling Sal she couldn't accept his promise ring—that she didn't want to marry him—had nearly sucked her heart out of her chest. He was such a kind man, just a year older than her. He'd had such beautiful dreams for their life. A house near the beach. Three kids. Two dogs. Dinner together around the table every night. A quiet life.

It had all sounded so wonderfully stable, so fantastically secure.

But she didn't love him.

Oh, how she cared for Sal. But after a year of dating, she'd realized he could never be more than a dear friend. A trusted confidant.

But she'd had those things with Will, too. So she'd known what she shared with Sal wasn't enough to build a life together. But the Gumbles had been just like family for six years. And breaking Sal's heart, refusing his proposal, meant that some things would have to change. If she said no, family dinners around the Gumble table would be awkward, at best. Time with Will at his home would always be tense. Abuelita's hugs would be strained.

Saying no would change everything Jess loved about her life.

So she'd contemplated saying yes. Jess had taken Sal's ring with a promise to think about it.

That night, she'd sat in Will's little Toyota, a block from her house, and showed him his great-grandmother's diamond.

"Did you say yes?" Will's eyes were so narrow that she couldn't make out any of the chocolate brown usually filled with laughter.

"No."

"Then why do you have the ring?" She didn't need to see his eyes to feel their accusation.

Her stomach lurched, and she covered her face with her hands. "I just couldn't tell him no. I said I'd think about it." Tears rolled down her cheeks, and she hiccuped against the spasms racking her chest. "What was I supposed to say? We've been dating almost a year. I don't want to hurt him."

Looking across the center console, she willed his hand to reach over and hold hers, but it stayed on his jean-clad leg, balled into a tight fist, the muscles in his forearms tense and sharply defined. His eyes looked straight forward through the windshield to the Gugenburgs' mailbox. His Adam's apple bobbed in his skinny neck.

"Say something." She hated the way panic took over her voice.

"He's my brother." His tone was flat and cold,

and she shivered in the warm May air that filtered through the open windows. "What do you want me to say?"

"I don't know. Just...something."

Will shoved a hand through his unruly hair. "I don't know what to say." His other fist bounced on his knee next to the steering wheel. "I mean, I want you to be happy. And Sal, too. So if you think marrying him will make both of you happy..."

"No." Though quiet, her word sliced through the car like the Jaws of Life.

"Jess, what do you want?"

"I don't want to hurt him, and I don't want to make things weird between me and your family, and I don't—"

Will held up his hand and looked her right in the eye. "That's what you *don't* want. What *do* you want?"

She wiped away the tears that streamed down her cheeks. "I want everything to stay the same between us."

"Why would it change?" The knuckles of his fist turned white as his jaw worked hard to get the words out.

"Will you still be my best friend if I marry Sal?" Her lungs cried for air as she waited for Will's reply.

His face twisted with a pain she couldn't pinpoint, but he inhaled sharply through his nose and said, "It's after your curfew. I should get you home."

"Will you pick me up in the morning for school?"

"I'll be there."

But he hadn't. That night had been the last time she saw Will, through tears and smeared mascara. She had whispered a good-night and run up the steps into her father's waiting embrace.

Now she could hear Will's heart thumping steadily beneath her ear, his comfort more powerful than any she'd known. What was this connection that drew her to him, while her head screamed warnings of the dangerous undertow?

She couldn't afford to be sucked under, to believe he was by her side to stay. It would only bring a broken heart, and she could ill afford another one. After her mom left, and her great-aunt Eva moved away, Will had bruised what little was left.

Still she held on to him, let him brush away her tears with even strokes of his thumb and soft words of encouragement. Pressing her nose into his neck, she breathed in his scent. He smelled of earth and mud and hard work, and she tightened her hold around him.

With a crooked forefinger, he tilted her chin until she had no choice but to meet his gaze. She let out a little gasp as he ran the pad of his thumb over the corner of her lip.

His other hand rested in the hollow at her waist, holding her gently in place.

Not that she was pulling away.

Her feet had grown roots, her eyes only able to focus on the dim outline of his lips. His jaw tightened for a long moment, pulling them taut. Then he relaxed but not into a smile.

Every vein in her body thrummed as he leaned closer and closer. Every inch seemed a mile, far too long before he'd reach her. But when he did, it was a perfect fit.

The war between her head and her heart forgotten for the moment, she pressed against him, wishing she could bottle that moment and save it for a lifetime. She was safe. She was home. And her heart was whole, if only for a second.

The softness of his T-shirt under her hands and the silkiness of his lips on hers effectively wrapped her in a cocoon of joy.

It was everything she'd always known it would be. Gentle and wild. Soft and full. Tender and untamed.

It was also making her heart swell so much that she had to pull away to catch her breath.

Leaning her forehead against his shoulder, she gulped for air as he let his arms drop to his sides.

At a loss for words, she said the three words that always came back to haunt them. "You left me."

"I know." The regret in his voice was nearly tangible, and she waited for him to go on. He hadn't explained why he'd gone, or told her what a terrible mistake it had been. She'd been telling herself for years that she didn't want or need his excuses, but after that kiss, with her knees still trembling, she knew she'd been wrong.

Say something. Anything. Tell me why you left. Just say you wish you'd stayed.

Long minutes ticked by, in a pregnant silence. Each second twisted the knot in her stomach more, until she thought she'd be sick.

And then he spoke. "You should get some sleep, and I should take care of our guy."

Not the words she had hoped to hear.

Stepping back, she kept her head bowed and her eyes closed. It was easier not to see him leave again.

The unconscious man sprawled on the floor looked skinny, yet as Will scooped him over a shoulder, he grunted under the weight. But the unexpected strain as he carried his burden out of Jess's room was a welcome distraction.

He offered Jess a soft good-night and bolted for the door before he did something really stupid.

Like fall to his knees, beg her to forgive him

for his cowardice and plead with her to be part of his life again. Forever.

Oh, kissing her hadn't been a smart move. He'd known that the second before their lips touched. But he was tired of caring about making the smart decision. He just needed to have her in his arms, even for just a taste of perfection. To smell the sweetness of her hair and remember without regret how good they'd been for each other.

In her uncertainties, he'd been certain. In his stubbornness, she'd stayed levelheaded.

They balanced each other. Always had.

And the spark that he'd wondered might be there…well, there was no denying it now. Her touch was lightning and rain in one, setting him on fire and soothing him in the same moment.

He lumbered down an alley, weaving between buildings until he reached the far side of the big house. His passenger groaned when Will stepped into a deep hole, and he jammed his shoulder into the man's gut just because he was ticked off.

At this cartel. At the unknown men who were watching them. At himself.

At the fact that he could never kiss Jess again.

Will slung the man to the ground at the base of a building, and his back thudded against the wall.

Squatting in front of Jess's would-be attacker, Will glared hard into the slack-jawed face. But he didn't see the narrow chin, patchy beard or crooked nose of the man in front of him. He saw Sal, bags beneath bloodshot eyes, shoulders sagging after a sleepless night. Sal with his untamable hair and rakish grin on the day Will had come to pick him up from the county lockup.

Will had crossed his arms, leaned against the hood of the car and tried to look casual as Sal sauntered down the police station steps. "How was it?"

Sal shrugged. "They won't be selling season tickets anytime soon."

Swatting his big brother, Will said, "Seriously, man. Why'd you do it?"

Sal sat on the car and tilted his face toward the morning sun like a man who had been in solitary confinement for a year instead of in a cell overnight.

"You're an adult now. This is on your permanent record."

Sal nodded slowly, several ripples popping up on his forehead. "I guess so."

Will pushed an elbow into Sal's side. "So? Why'd you take the rap for me?"

Identical brown eyes locked in a silent stalemate. "Because Dad wasn't kidding when he said one more run-in with the cops and you'd be going to military school next year."

Searching for the right response, Will glared at his crossed arms. Sal was right. His dad had made the threat clear. It didn't matter if Will's juvenile rap sheet was made up of minor vandalism infractions. One more trip home in the back of a cop car and Will was bound for Texas and the Trident Military Academy, a private institute for young men. The headmaster was a retired navy SEAL and an old friend of their father's, and the school was supposed to be…intense. To say the least.

"You may make me want to pound you into the ground sometimes, but you're still my brother."

"You think I couldn't hack it at military school?" Will asked, as casually as he could manage, wondering what his brother really thought of him. When Sal looked at him, did he see nothing more than a reckless screwup, the way their father did?

"If you wanted to be there, I think you'd do just fine. But if you were sent there as a punishment? With Dad's friend riding roughshod over you every day? It wouldn't end well. I want better than that for you. Besides, Jess would kill me if I let you get sent away. For some inconceivable reason, she likes having you around, and I like having *her* around."

Will chuckled. That was the understatement of the century. His brother had been head over heels for Jess for at least a year. Everyone knew it.

Sal had taken the blame for an inappropriate message spray-painted on an overpass and saved

Will from the military academy. It was just one of a dozen times that Sal had saved him over the years and it had cemented in Will's mind the knowledge that he could never repay his brother. So he'd vowed to get his act together. At least until he was done with high school.

The unconscious man's head rolled, and he let out a low groan, bringing Will back to the present and the anger still boiling just beneath his skin.

It didn't matter how many times Will kissed Jess. She would never be his, because Sal deserved better. Even eighteen-year-old, selfish Will had known that. Twenty-eight-year-old Will, who had learned what brotherhood meant from men like L. T. Sawyer and Rock Waterstone and Luke Dunham, was sure of it. They laid down their lives for their SEAL brothers every day, and they'd taught him to do the same.

Will just had to get Jess out of here in one piece, and then he could forget about that kiss. And walk out of her life.

Until then, he had to know who this guy was. It was too dark for Will to be certain he could identify the intruder in the light of day. He could think of only one surefire way to keep the thug on the radar.

With a quick pop of Will's fist, the guy cried out, his head bouncing off the wall at his back before sagging to the side. The black eye would be easy for Jess and him to spot.

A grin crept across Will's face.

And it felt pretty good to give, too.

TEN

Will followed Sergio into the lab the next morning, his stomach a strange jumble of uncertainty. He'd dreamed of Jess during his short respite, but the smooth perfection of her profile in reality made his dream seem two-dimensional and black-and-white.

She was already at work, measuring teaspoons of white powder into a metal bowl. Her eyes didn't leave the measuring spoon, and she didn't pause to greet him.

"Morning," he said.

She gave a curt nod by way of reply, all the time mouthing the count of her measurements.

She looked about as eager to engage with him as he was to spend another muggy night in this pit.

Instead of addressing the elephant in the room, he slipped his apron over his head and snapped his gloves into place. "How can I help?"

Jess pointed to the air compressor in the corner. The round tank sat on four wheels, a motor, fan and dials attached to the top. "We'd better test that out and make sure it actually works."

He did as she asked, moving over to the machine, plugging it into the wall and turning it on. It sputtered, as old as everything else in the lab, but finally settled into a steady hum that competed with the air conditioner for supremacy in noise pollution.

Grabbing the nozzle at the end of the black rubber hose, Will pressed the lever. A stream of air released with a loud hiss and a jerk of the tube.

"Looks like it'll work to me."

Jess nodded and motioned for him to bring it over, the muscles in her neck visibly straining.

Sergio's eyes followed Will as he bent and rolled the machine across the floor, every third step earning a squeak from a wheel. When he reached her, she was scooping the mixed powder into one of the cleaned tear gas canisters. She weighed it on an electronic scale several times, and when she was satisfied, screwed the stopper and detonation mechanism into place. It looked like a miniature fire extinguisher, and it would work nearly the same way.

Will waited for Jess to say something, to break her silence as she worked. But with every tick of the clock on the wall, taking them closer to their date with El Jefe and the demonstration he demanded, she drew further away.

Finally, he reached for her, resting his hand on her back. She didn't flinch or push him off, so he leaned in a bit closer. "Jess, tell me what you're thinking."

She sighed and rubbed her gloved hands over her arms. "This is a precursor to what they want to do with the toxin." She shot a glance at Manuel, who was watching her as closely as Sergio was. "What if this is enough? What if they can use this to unleash death on an entire camp?"

"They won't risk it without you."

"But they have me."

"Not for long." Will hoped his smile masked the uncertainty that burned through his chest.

Her nose wrinkled and her lips pursed. "We only have three days."

"Which means we'll be gone in two."

"How?"

Such a simple question with no simple answer. If he knew how, they'd already be gone. But jumping the wall, knowing there were snares out there, would be stupid. Doing it with a cartel on their tail would be a suicide mission.

They had to get free with a head start. And preferably an extraction plan in place.

"I'm still working on it."

He mentally ticked off the intel they'd collected so far.

He was getting a pretty good sense of the guard rotations. They worked eight-hour shifts, changing at midnight, eight in the morning and four in the afternoon, never leaving the front gate unattended. The guardhouses at the top of the wall were a little harder to gauge. Sometimes they were occupied, and sometimes he just couldn't tell. Of course, there were also a hundred other thugs roaming the compound who couldn't be accounted for at any given point in time.

He and Jess had seen the map of the area. He hadn't had time to memorize it, but he'd gained a pretty good sense of where they were and how far west they needed to go.

But he also knew there was something waiting for them on the other side of those walls. Whatever it was could be better than what they faced inside. Or it could be a whole lot worse.

It was a risk they were going to have to take.

And the big question still loomed. How were they going to get the Morsyni out of the lab? He glanced at the window, which had been shut by someone else in the past couple days. If whoever had closed it connected the open window to his absence from his room two nights prior, this lab was going to be under surveillance 24/7.

"I'm going to figure something out," he whispered. "I promise."

She nodded, picking up the can and checking the small dial at the base of the neck. "Turn that on for me?" Her chin indicated the compressor.

He did as she asked, as she squeezed the release handle of the container. If there had been any air pressure inside, it would have released everything inside the tin.

"All right." She squeezed her eyes closed and bit the inside of her cheek. "I want you to put the nozzle against the opening here." She tapped it with her finger. "When I tell you to, start the air. But whatever you do, don't pull it away until I let go of the handle. Got it?"

Will nodded, and Sergio and Manuel leaned forward.

"Now!" Jess said, and he rammed the compressor's nozzle into place. It all seemed to take just a second before she released the handle and shoved in a pin to keep it from accidentally going off.

If the pin was pulled and the handle held down, then the canister would release. Just like a grenade.

For this trial run, with a nontoxic mix inside, it was safe. But it wouldn't be when Juan Carlos returned.

Just as Will pushed the machine into a corner

and out of the way, the lab door blew open, revealing a slim man. With a black eye.

Jess glanced up, but clearly didn't recognize him.

"Ready?" His voice was gruff. "El Jefe is waiting for your demonstration."

"Almost." Jess picked up the canister and looked into Will's face.

This was his only chance to warn her before they marched outside. Turning his back to their guards and El Jefe's lackey, Will leaned to push the compressor farther into the corner. In a barely audible whisper, he said, "The man with the black eye was your visitor last night. Be careful."

Jess was going to be sick.

Doubling over, she leaned her forehead against the cool counter, gasping the thick air even as it threatened to choke her.

"Hey. It's okay." Will rubbed her back in perfect circles.

But it wasn't okay. It was all too much.

Forced to do a test run for the release of a toxin that would kill hundreds, maybe thousands. The man who had stolen into her room in the dead of night only feet away.

A sweeping, sure knowledge that she wasn't going to make Christmas with her dad.

Tears pooled in her eyes, and she knuckled them away.

She wouldn't let herself break down.

She *wouldn't*.

After gulping three quick breaths and swallowing as many hiccuping sobs, she pressed her gloved hands to her cheeks and squared her shoulders.

Her dad had taught her to be a good sailor, both on the water and off. And right now that required a rigid backbone and a stiff upper lip. Forcing her fists down to her sides, she shrugged off Will's hand at her elbow.

"Let's just get this over with."

"All right." He motioned for her to take the lead. "After you."

She marched past the man with a black eye without even acknowledging him. He glared at her, his hand absently rubbing the back of his head. If she had her wrench, she'd remind him just who he had tried to mess with.

But the black eye made her grin. Though the room had been dark, she was pretty sure that he hadn't had it when Will had hoisted him over a shoulder and carried him away. Will had gotten in at least one good jab.

She followed a narrow alley all the way to the courtyard, Will, Manuel, Sergio and Mr. Shiner trailing. Will carried the can filled with the improvised, harmless compound. But every time Jess envisioned the container filled with the Morsyni, her chest tightened and her hands shook.

These people had no idea the power they were dealing with.

"Welcome. Welcome to our little party." El Jefe spread his arms wide, indicating the crude circle of forty or so men. Most sported hands and clothes dirty from their labor, but their eyes were bright with curiosity. "Arturo, thank you for bringing our guests of honor."

The man with the black eye nodded in reply.

El Jefe motioned for Arturo to join him, and Sergio herded Jess and Will in the same direction. "We've been looking forward to your demonstration all day, Jessica."

She cringed at the name, one she'd been fighting for most of her life. Everyone assumed that Jess was short for the common name. But she'd been called Jessalynn after her mother, Lynn. Just another in a long list of selfish decisions her mom had made.

Jess had been trying to get rid of that reminder since her mother had taken off. Since Lynn McCoy had decided that being married to a sailor too often deployed on a submarine wasn't always fun. Since she'd decided that her twelve-year-old daughter wasn't worth taking along.

Even when someone called her by the wrong

name, Jess was reminded of what her mother had done. Lynn hadn't come back, but Jess was stuck with her name. Even publishing her research under her nickname hadn't kept the constant reminders at bay.

"Let's not keep everyone waiting." El Jefe's high-pitched voice brought the low rumble of the crowd to an immediate halt, every eye turning in her direction.

Reaching for the canister, Jess took a deep breath and begged heavenward for an intervention. If ever the DEA was going to find them, this would be as good a time as any. *God, if You want to send help...*

She listened for the sound of choppers or an explosion at the front gate. None came. So she lifted the can and stretched her arm back to launch it.

"Wait." Arturo waved a clean hand, free from the grime his compatriots wore. "He should do it." A slender hand clapped Will's shoulder, and if Jess had a guess, she figured Will's lurch forward was an exaggerated response.

El Jefe's eyes grew wide, his frown turning into a wicked smile. "*Sí.* Yes. Let's do that." Pointing at Will, he said, "You do it."

Her breath caught, and she almost choked. They hadn't talked about how to release it. Not that it was terribly difficult to figure out, but what if he didn't hold it high enough and ended up spraying himself in the face? They'd quickly figure out that he wasn't the brilliant scientist his cover touted him to be.

Will stepped forward, his brown eyes blank, his face completely passive as he held his palms up in front of him. She mimicked pressing the button next to the nozzle, and he gave a quick nod. Then she mouthed, *Toss it hard.*

With every eye on them, it was all she could risk.

He took the stage, walking into the middle of the circle with the confidence of an Oscar winner. He made a show of every step, as if he'd been throwing death cans every day of his life.

Every head tilted down to stare at the billowing white cloud spiraling out of the flying can. Then they looked up as the cloud wafted in the breeze before slowly falling to the earth. Several men held out their hands to catch the haze. It vanished in their grasps, leaving only a faint trace on their shoulders and heads.

El Jefe clapped three times in slow succession before the entire assembly broke out in applause and excited whoops.

"Very good. Very good." He turned to Arturo, his face twisting with the joy of menace. "We will be ready when Juan Carlos arrives."

El Jefe and Arturo spit out several excited lines

of Spanish, their hands cutting through the air as their volume grew.

Suddenly El Jefe turned on Jess. "How far will the cloud spread?"

"As far as the wind takes it," she answered.

"And anyone who comes in contact with it will die?"

She closed her eyes. They'd distorted and twisted all her research for their own gain. She'd spent almost three years studying this toxin to find a *cure* for its effects, something to neutralize it and keep it from killing anyone else. And they'd taken that from her and were going to use it to destroy another cartel.

The other compound might not be filled with "good guys," but they were still human. They deserved better than a painful, prolonged death.

"They will die?" El Jefe's voice dropped to a growl.

"Yes."

She had a sick feeling that she and Will wouldn't be far behind those other poor souls.

"Very, very good."

Will glared at the evil little man. What kind of warped mind took pleasure in plotting the demise of hundreds of lives?

It shouldn't surprise him. Will had seen plenty of evil in his six years on the SEAL teams. It was part of the job. L. T. Sawyer, the CO of his platoon, had described the job of a SEAL as a "sin eater." They faced the worst, the most heinous evil in the world. And then they removed that sin so that others could be free.

Just part of the job.

But it never got easier.

Especially face-to-face with the evil and unable to do more than wait for the right opportunity to take action. If he jumped the gun or chose the wrong moment, Jess's life would be on the line. His, too.

El Jefe was still rattling on about his big plans for Juan Carlos's arrival, but Arturo's gaze had settled heavily onto Jess. Her entire body shivered under the weight of it, and he knew she felt it. Her hazel eyes were hollow, haunted by the situation at hand.

Before he even realized what he was doing, Will reached for her arm to offer a reassuring squeeze. But when his hand was only halfway there, Arturo's eyes narrowed. Will aborted the movement and ran his fingers through his hair instead, but the other man's scowl didn't change.

Like volcanoes erupting, the thug's eyes shot fire through the air. Will knew he should back down. He knew that a mild-mannered scientist would bow his head and take a couple steps back.

In the face of such danger, a lab rat wasn't liable to step toward the threat.

But Will wasn't a scientist. And he certainly wasn't mild-mannered.

Cocking his chin up a notch, he stared hard into Arturo's stunned eyes.

The bully frowned and dropped his gaze quickly. He was used to having men cower in front of him, but Will wasn't going to do it. Not anymore. He'd played their game long enough— sneaking through the shadows and caring for Jess mostly under the dark of night. It was time to stand up for them both.

"Manuel, take them back to the lab." El Jefe, still bent over the used canister, dismissed them with a wave of his hand.

The guard did as he was told, corralling them down the alley, but he was too busy looking over his shoulder at the conversation still going on in the courtyard to pay Will and Jess much mind. Arturo and El Jefe continued their animated discussion about the successful demonstration they would take credit for as soon as Juan Carlos arrived. And from what they said, Will gleaned that he'd be there sooner than they had expected.

With a hand on her trembling back, Will ushered Jess to the far corner of the lab. He clasped her hands in his, not even bothering to check the level of the counter that might hide them from Manuel's gaze if he ever looked away from his boss.

Jess gazed up at him, blinking rapidly, her eyelashes covered with a fine sheen of tears. Cupping her cheeks with his hands, Will brushed his thumbs across the top of her cheeks, stealing away the moisture collecting there.

"Hey, tell me what's going on in your head."

Her chin quivered, but she bit into her cheeks, screwing up her jaw against the telltale sign. She swallowed three times, but still didn't speak.

"I can't read your mind." He stooped to her level while he smoothed the top of her hair in long strokes. "Let me help you. What's going on in there?"

"It's going to wor—" her voice caught on an unnamed emotion, but she twisted her face as she fought to finish "—work."

"What is?"

"The Morsyni. The release mechanism. When they try to use it, it's going to work. Even without me. And I'll be responsible for it when that happens."

Will's stomach ached as if he hadn't eaten in days. He'd give anything if he could take that weight from her shoulders. But she'd have to carry this experience with her. There was no getting around it. "Don't think like that. They're responsible for the actions they take, not you. They're trying to use you as a pawn."

"I hate chess."

A laugh bubbled up in his chest, and he had to cover it with a cough, pressing his fist to his mouth. He'd seen her playing with her dad one time, and she'd gotten so upset that she threw the board and all the little marble pieces on the floor. Of course, she'd been thirteen at the time.

This Jess had just as much spirit.

"It's a stupid game, and I'm really bad at it. But even I know that a pawn is the lowest piece, and I am not the lowest piece on the board right now." The shimmering in her eyes vanished, replaced by a determined fire.

"Good. You're ready for a fight. Because we're about to get one." He glanced toward Manuel, who had left the door open and wandered back in the direction of the courtyard. "It sounds like Juan Carlos might have moved up his visit. I think he's going to be here sooner than we thought, and he's most likely going to want to see what we've been up to. So we've got to look ready for him."

Jess nodded, crossing her arms over her stomach and holding her elbows. "The attack?"

"As far as I know it's still planned for three days from now."

She let out a low sigh.

"Maybe we can use Juan Carlos's arrival to cover our absence."

God, let Amy and her DEA team find my GPS signal. We don't have much time. And we can't beat these guys through the jungle.

Jess gave another silent nod, and he wished he could trust his own words as easily. It wouldn't be quite so simple to get away with Arturo's eyes watching their every move, and that was before Will even thought about how they'd get to Panama City.

"Don't worry. We'll be out of here on our way back to the States long before they can lay a hand on the toxin."

His words didn't even come close to convincing himself, and the doubtful look in Jess's eyes suggested they hadn't done much to sway her, either.

ELEVEN

For days in captivity the hours had been dragging by, each second a year, each hour a decade of mental torment. But when Jess knew that the moment for their escape had nearly arrived, time seemed to vanish before her, no minute long enough to make plans and cover their tracks. In the meantime her hands moved without pausing, preparing the pressurized canisters to carry the Morsyni for Juan Carlos's planned attack.

Over and over, she chanted in her mind, *This is not for real. This is not for real.*

They would take the Morsyni with them.

Tonight.

No one would be hurt. She'd be responsible for no one's death. That reassurance kept her moving as Will worked in silence by her side.

He looked as if he was working on a similar project, cleaning the release valves. But instead he was playing with a six-inch piece of wire, bending and folding it until it disappeared around a button on the cuff of his shirt.

Sergio had watch duty, but kept his ear pressed against the door, likely listening for the commotion that would mean the boss had arrived. Finally, the blades of a helicopter cut the air, louder than a tornado.

When the pilot turned off the chopper's engine, the slowly subsiding roar of the rotors was replaced by exuberant cheers that reached them as though the building didn't even have walls.

Juan Carlos was either extravagantly loved or infinitely feared.

Sergio glared at Will and Jess, as though it was entirely their fault that he wasn't outside to watch the spectacle. He paced the front of the room, swinging his gun back and forth and mumbling to himself. Finally, he barked something and left, slamming the metal door behind him. After a short pause, a loud click secured the outside lock on the best exit from the room.

"Hope there's not a fire," Jess said wryly. Will gave an obligatory chuckle. "What are you doing?" She was so used to keeping her voice low that the words were barely audible.

He looked innocent as he held up his sleeve. "You like it?"

"What's it for?"

"We're going to have to break into the lab tonight. They keep it padlocked when we're not in here, and I don't think I'll be able to get the keys before we need back in."

"Where'd you learn to do that?"

"Huh?" One of his eyebrows flattened.

"Pick a lock."

He shrugged. "Just part of the job. You pick things up all over the world from everyone you meet. I can blow up a brick of C-4, order a cup of coffee in Iraq, fly a Blackhawk. Well…in a pinch." He gave her a saucy wink. "They'd never give me a license to fly one after I nearly took the last one into the side of a mountain when the pilots were shot."

Not for the first time in the past week, she wondered who this man really was.

He was confident, but not obnoxiously cocky. He gave her orders as if he was used to having them obeyed. Even worse, they were always the best thing to do. There wasn't an unsure bone in his body, and she'd begun to rely on that.

"Luke taught me how to pick a lock his first week on our team. He said it helped him relieve stress." Will reached for a can. "It's kind of like the job. Searching in the dark for the one thing that will make sense out of everything else that's going on. Most guys watch TV or get on the computer or call their families when we have downtime. Luke, he sits on his bunk and picks padlocks."

"Who's Luke?"

"My best friend." Will didn't look up from the release valve in his hands, but his words were a kick to her stomach.

Of course he had a best friend. She had good friends, too. Several of them, actually. Friends from school and women she'd met while volunteering at Pacific Coast House, a safe home for women and children who had suffered domestic abuse. Ashley and Staci, a pair of sisters-in-law who ran the home, had become surrogate family to Jess before her dad returned to San Diego and his new post as the XO of the base at Coronado.

But somehow, even after all these years of radio silence, she couldn't bring herself to call anyone but Will her *best* friend.

Maybe it was because he'd so magnificently violated the title that she couldn't easily give it out again.

Or maybe—and she had a twinge in her stomach that suggested this might be the case—it was just because she'd always hoped he'd come back and want the moniker again.

"He sounds…nice." Was there a more inappropriate word? The guy picked locks to relieve stress. He was a navy SEAL. He was probably anything but just plain old *nice*.

Will chuckled, deep in his throat. "Luke is… Luke. He's a good guy. The kind you want by your side in a firefight."

"And how many have you been in together?"

Will's hands stopped moving, and he shot her a glance out of the side of his eye. "Why do you want to know?"

She shrugged, suddenly terribly uncomfortable with the direction of this conversation and all her thoughts about herself and Luke and especially Will. "Never mind. I know better than to ask." Even though her dad had taught her not to, she'd made the mistake of asking a SEAL once about his recent mission. She'd let a grad school friend talk her into going to a pub that everyone knew SEALs hung out at, and when one started chatting her up, she'd asked where he had been deployed. He'd drawn up tighter than a cheapskate's purse strings. SEALs didn't talk about what they did. The mystery was part of their appeal to the women who frequented that pub.

And anyway, Will's missions were absolutely none of her business.

He scratched his chin, his fingernails rasping the week-old beard growing there. "We've been through enough for me to know he's the guy I want watching my six."

"You trust him, then?"

"Of course." Will's voice raised in an unspoken question as he gazed straight into her eyes, as if he was trying to read whatever was written on her heart. "Do you trust *me?* To get you out of here, I mean."

The weight of his gaze, or maybe his question, was too much for her to handle. She turned away, staring at the point where her hands rested on the sleek black counter. She pressed them flat to keep them from trembling as a flood of emotions washed through her.

"Jess?"

"What do you want me to say?"

He stabbed his fingers through his hair, leaving a resilient section standing on end, before scrubbing his face with his palms. "I don't know. I guess I just hoped that by now you'd trust me on this mission."

"I know you can handle the mission stuff." The words popped out before she even realized they were on the tip of her tongue, but she knew immediately that they were true. "I can see that you're a good SEAL. I know you'll figure out a way for us to get out of here. It's just the rest…"

"What rest? Ten years ago?"

"Will, you were the *best* friend I'd ever had. I told you everything. Even about my mom leaving. I never told anyone else. Not even Sal knew that she didn't tell me she was going and never came back for me."

Will's swallow was thick and audible in the sudden silence. "I didn't realize I was the only one you'd told."

"I know. I didn't want to tell you, but you asked. And no one ever asked. Everyone who knew just knew. My dad. Great-aunt Eva. And everyone else seemed to think they weren't allowed to bring it up in front of me. I don't think your mom even knew the whole story. She just took me in like I was one of her own." Stupid tears welled up in the corners of Jess's eyes, and she pressed the heels of her hands there to keep a breakdown at bay. Why did she always cry when she talked about her mom? Usually they were tears of frustration, but these were something else. Something deeper.

This was neither the time nor the place to dig into whatever that might be.

Will rubbed her shoulder, but she shrugged off his touch, the sensation too much to tolerate in her already hyperaware state.

"You were the most stable family I had. And then you just left. No note. No call. No nothing. For ten years. It was just like mom all over again. Like you'd decided I wasn't worth sticking around for."

"I know. And I am so sorry." His voice dropped, pain and another emotion she couldn't identify woven through every word.

"I don't want your apologies," she snapped, then cringed and pressed her hand to her forehead, letting out a sigh between tight lips. Swiping her hand beneath her drippy nose, she took a stabilizing breath. "Sorry. It's just that every time I see you, all I feel is this terrible hole in my heart where my best friend is supposed to be." She pressed her fist to the hollow in the center of her chest. "And all I know is that you're just like her."

His face fell at her harsh words. "Oh, Jess, don't say that."

"How else am I supposed to feel? Am I supposed to forget what you did just because you showed up this time when I needed you? Just because I needed to be rescued and you could help?"

"No, of course—"

"And you didn't come back because you wanted to. You came because my dad sent you." Will opened his mouth, clearly ready to argue one or both of those points, but she waved her finger in the air to keep him quiet. "I mean, I'm glad that you're here, and not just because you're trained and capable of getting us out of here. It really is good to see you again. And I trust that you can do your job. I just…"

Oh, the words were there, but not. They were so close she could taste them, but they were bitter and hostile, and she wanted to spit them out, but couldn't find the way. So she swallowed them.

Just as she'd done with every word she'd wanted to say to her mother for sixteen years.

A muscle in Will's jaw jumped as Jess's voice trailed off, his mouth working in silent deliberation.

"I don't know what I want from you, but right now, I just want to get home in time for Christmas," she finally said. "I want to sit in my dad's living room and give him a fishing pole. I want to eat his dry turkey, mushy stuffing and soggy pumpkin pie. I want him to hug me and promise me that this will never happen again. I want to spend my favorite holiday with the one person in my life who has never let me down."

"I'm going to do everything I can to make that happen, but..." Will let out a strong breath through his nose. "I owe you an explanation."

"Does it even matter?" She wanted it not to. She wanted that so much, and she prayed that saying the words would make it so. "You've risked your life for me at least a dozen times in the last week. Thank you for that. I appreciate it. But I'm not sure I can ever forgive you."

Will had been shot before, but that hadn't hurt as much as this. It stung just to breathe, and it had nothing to do with the stale air. He rubbed a hand over his chest, trying to clear what was blocking his throat. Except he couldn't rub off the words that sank into his skin like a tattoo.

Still, his apology was incomplete. She deserved the truth—at least what was his to tell.

"I was scared, okay?"

Her head shot around faster than a hummingbird.

"I was a stupid kid, and I was scared of losing you."

"So you did what? Made sure you lost me on your own terms? How'd that work out for you?" Bitterness dripped from every syllable, her eyes sparking with anger and frustration. She'd said she didn't want justifications, but the questions on her face flashed loud and clear.

At least she was showing emotion. And anger he could handle. It was the tears she'd had just minutes before that sent his stomach into a dive. She'd had ten years to let bitterness fester, and he didn't blame her for not forgiving him.

After all these years, he hadn't quite figured out how to forgive himself.

Inhaling deeply, he hunted for the right response.

"I didn't know how to be both Sal's brother and your best friend. I couldn't hope you'd say yes and no at the same time. It was like being torn in two."

There were no maps for this kind of thing. Maps he could read. Directions he could follow.

A compass and the stars could get him anywhere he wanted to go. But no one had ever plotted the words to say when words weren't enough.

"You're not making any sense, Will."

"I know." He shifted his weight to his other leg, suddenly craving a five-mile run in the sand almost as much as hearing her say his name again. "I didn't understand then and I still don't entirely. It was all too much."

"What was too much?"

He sighed, glaring at the ceiling and begging for the right words to make her understand. "I think I was in love you. I was just too young, too insecure to realize it. I just knew I could *not* watch you marry my brother. So instead of telling you what I was feeling—or even dealing with my feelings at all—I took the coward's way out."

"I don't…I don't understand. That last night in your car. Why didn't you tell me?"

"And have you do what? Ask me why? Suggest that I didn't want you to be a permanent part of my family?" He grabbed onto his hair at the roots and yanked. Pain helped him focus, and in that moment, he desperately needed help to keep his words on track and his voice calm. "You would have made me tell you. And at the time, I didn't even know why. But I knew that Sal's ring on your finger was going to change things between us. I didn't want that."

She closed her eyes and bit her bottom lip, making it red and plump, and sending his mind where it had no business going, recalling recent memories of his lips pressed to hers.

"So why did you stay away?"

"Because."

"That's the best you can come up with? I thought you were smarter than that. Most SEALs are."

His skin suddenly felt too tight, and his blood was pounding too hard, nearly drowning out her taunt.

"I mean, you knew I turned Sal down, right?"

"I heard. About a year later."

"So why not call me then? Or send me an email? Two lines. 'Jess, I'm okay. I'll be back.' Boom. Done. Is that too much to ask?"

"Right about then, I wasn't very proud of the man that I'd become. I was doing my best to live up to every negative stereotype a navy man could acquire. I wasn't good enough for you, and I knew it."

"What changed?"

He refused to analyze if her question suggested that he was worthy of her now. Because it didn't matter. Even if they both wanted to be together, Sal's continued feelings for her stood between them like a sentry.

"I met a couple guys. L.T. and Rock. They're

SEALs and men of integrity, and, man, I wanted to be like them."

Her face scrunched up. "L.T.—Tristan Sawyer?"

Will paused, examining the subtle shifting of her eyes. "Yes."

"I know him. Well, not really. But I know his wife, Staci, and his sister, Ashley."

Will shook his head, his worlds colliding so fast that he had to hold on to his chin to keep his head from falling off. "Of course you do. From the shelter?"

"Do you know them?"

"Well, way before she was L.T.'s wife, Staci almost got me run over by a van in front of Pacific Coast House."

Jess's hand shot forward to grab his arm. "Were you hurt?"

"I said 'almost.'" But he didn't mind the tender grip on his forearm or the concern wrinkling her forehead.

Taking a little step forward, he wrapped his hand around hers, holding it in place. Her gaze shot to the point of contact, but she didn't try to pull away.

"I'm glad." She blinked and licked her lips, still focused on his hand. "That you weren't run over, I mean."

"Me, too." He stared at her, his attention entirely consumed by her. She smelled of plastic and rubber and the lab, and despite the lack of sleep, her eyes were bright, her cheeks pink with life. He reached his free hand to her face, running his knuckles over the satin of her skin.

Finally, she looked up and let out a long sigh. "I'm still mad you."

"You should be."

"Why are you making it harder for me to stay angry?"

He shrugged, giving her a gentle smirk. "I'm not trying to."

"I know." She looked away, but didn't dislodge his finger, which had stopped under her chin. "That's what's making it hard. You used to pass blame off whenever you could. But you're not that guy anymore, are you?"

Risking another little step toward her, he fully invaded her space. Her feet didn't move, but her breath caught on a sudden intake as her eyes grew wide.

"Jessalynn, I knew I didn't deserve you back then, and I'm not arrogant enough to think that I do now. But I'm trying hard to be a better man. Whatever that looks like. Every day. And today, that means that you can count on me. I won't leave you again."

"Does that mean that we'll be friends when

we get back to San Diego? Will we pick up right where we left off?"

It would have been so easy to say yes. It would also have been a lie. Now that he knew he loved her—and that he could never hurt his brother by trying for a relationship with her—how could he stand being by her side but never holding her? Being her best friend but knowing that he'd never be anything more?

He bit back the easy answer in favor of an honest one. "I don't know. I don't think it's that simple. But if you need me, I will be there for you. All right?"

Her eyes grew wide, deep and stormy as the ocean. Her apron brushed against his, and his breath stirred the chestnut strands that had escaped the rubber band in her hair. Had he stepped closer? Apparently so.

But not close enough.

When his shoe bumped into hers, he paused. Then leaned in a little more.

This was a terrible idea. He had no business getting so near to her. Again. It was bound to lead to the same place it had last time.

But his promise deserved to be sealed with a kiss. And any good military man knew better than to argue with protocol.

Slipping both arms around her back, he pulled her all the way against him. She squeaked and pressed her hands to his chest. The hum in his ears started low and slow, building with every second as he memorized her face. The freckles sprinkled over her nose hadn't changed, but the fine lines on either side of her smile were new. Her lips were pink and smooth and hanging open just enough to show off her adorably crooked front tooth. Long lashes fluttered over her eyes, never lifting much past the level of his nose.

Maybe she was as mesmerized by his lips as he was by hers.

Could they have had ten years of this? If he'd just talked with Sal? If he'd been honest with himself? If he hadn't been a coward?

Just how much he'd thrown away, Will would never know.

But for a second, he set aside regrets and just let himself enjoy the moment.

Only a breath away, he whispered, "I won't leave you again."

Jess rose on her toes, pushing their lips together with a hunger and passion that made the rest of the world vanish. The lab, the toxin, the mission. All of it disappeared as her fingers curled over the edge of his apron.

She was like thunder in his arms, powerfully uncontainable, and he couldn't let go for fear that he'd never capture anything like it again.

Taking back control, he deepened the kiss, enjoying the way her hands wandered to his neck and the hollow behind his ear. Cool fingertips danced along the back of his jaw, scraping against his whiskers, until his entire body trembled. Or was it Jess who was shaking?

Where he stopped and she started had turned fuzzy as his head spun.

He couldn't breathe, didn't want to if it meant this kiss had to end.

Jess fell heavily against him, her legs seemingly unable to hold her upright a moment longer. He pulled back just long enough to suck in oxygen and scoop her onto the counter before catching the corner of her mouth again.

She clung to his arms as if they were a lifeline and she was drowning.

Maybe she was. Maybe they both were.

All he knew for sure was that it was the sweetest drowning he'd ever known.

But this had to be the last time.

He pulled away, hoping to end the torture before it was too late, before he couldn't form a coherent reason why it couldn't be like this for the rest of forever.

Her lips were rosy and swollen and trembling. They parted in a silent breath, and he was completely undone.

* * *

Jess couldn't breathe. Will had effectively sucked all the air out of the room, out of her life. But she needed him, needed his strength and his heart, way more than she needed oxygen. So when he pulled away, she clamped her eyes closed against the immediate sense of loss.

She felt like vapor, flying in every direction, uncontained and unrestrained. Pressing her lips together, she tried to collect her thoughts, but it was as useless as grabbing for a balloon caught in the wind.

Not even the edge of the counter digging into the back of her thighs could bring her to the present.

And then his lips found hers again.

Settling his lean hips between her knees, he cupped the back of her head, cradling and protecting her and making her forget every reason for her bitterness.

She couldn't find the right grasp on him, so her hands roamed over his arms, across the long muscles of his shoulders and up his neck. The short hairs at his collar tickled her fingers, so she played with them. A deep and satisfied groan filled her, and it took her a moment to realize it had come from him.

Somehow, someday, she was going to make him make that sound again.

But before she could even attempt it, the heavy padlock on the door clicked.

Her stomach jolted, but Will was faster, sliding her down his front until her wobbling legs had to support her weight.

"Be ready tonight. I'll come for you after midnight."

Her brain had turned to mush, and his words didn't make any sense. "Where are we going?"

"Over the wall."

Everything snapped together, and she pulled herself upright, heels together and shoulders level. Just as the heavy metal door swung in, she ran her hand over her ponytail and tried to straighten any flyaway wisps.

It was too late for a complete overhaul, and she just hoped she didn't look as if she'd just been kissed. Thoroughly.

El Jefe and Arturo sauntered in, shoulder to shoulder, then parted to reveal a tall, sleek man, whose gray suit shimmered in late-afternoon remnants of sunlight. His eyes could have pierced solid cement. He ran a palm over his oil-slicked hair before using two ringed fingers to pinch his lips.

Jess's heart skipped a beat at the intensity of his perusal.

When he lowered his hand, he cracked his knuckles one at a time, each a deliberate action.

"Hello. My name is Juan Carlos Reyes Alvarez." His gaze followed a sharp path between Will and Jess. "You'll be avenging my brother's death. I want them to suffer."

TWELVE

Will was still sick from the short interview with the cartel's kingpin. Juan Carlos had a smugness about him that curdled what little was in Will's stomach, and the man's complete lack of regard for human life made Will's skin crawl.

He wasn't just a guy who did bad things.

He was a man who took pleasure in wreaking havoc and death.

And he'd convinced himself that what he was doing was the right and true thing.

Will sat on the edge of his bed, rubbing his hands slowly together, the hiss of skin against skin the only sound in his room.

Juan Carlos hadn't said much more after his formal introduction. Except, "We are so pleased to have two such astute scientists with us. For the time being."

Jess had jumped at the unspoken threat of those four little words, and Will had fought every urge in his body not to scoop her up and run away at that moment. Forget the toxin. Forget the armed guards and whatever those booby traps were outside the wall. Forget the rival cartel and the danger of the surrounding jungle.

None of it mattered if Jess was in harm's way.

But acting brash wasn't going to save either of them.

So he had swallowed every protective instinct and stood his ground, just a little in front of her, slightly more in the path of Arturo's gun, if he decided to use it.

Behind closed eyes, Will played out every possible scenario he could come up with for their escape. Ideally, he'd go to the lab alone, pick up the powder still stored in the refrigerator, then pick up Jess at her cell. He'd give her the toxin, and he'd take her mattress, which he'd sling over the barbed wire and glass atop the wall near the compound's northwest corner. He'd boost Jess up and over, and he'd follow.

They'd be free, if they could avoid the danger represented by those red marks on the map. He could see their positions on the map in his mind's eye. He just didn't know for sure what they were.

And an unknown in this scenario could mean the difference between escape and death.

"God, I'm at a loss here. You know that I am. I need Your help." The prayer seemed to bounce around the empty room, and with a sigh Will leaned his elbows onto his knees.

When he'd first met L.T. and Rock, he'd known there was something special about them. It wasn't just the never-say-die attitude or spirit of brotherhood on the teams. It wasn't only their hard work or integrity. They wore peace like body armor and hope like a helmet.

After a long first year on the teams, Will had realized he needed that same peace and hope if he ever wished to make it out of his service in the navy intact. It wasn't about fear of physical injury or being a sin eater. It was about knowing that with God on his side the rest would take care of itself.

But just now, that peace seemed like a distant memory.

Whether he felt peace or not, this was about rescuing Jess and keeping his promise.

He'd get her home by Christmas.

With another silent prayer for protection and stealth, he stood, marched to his window and hoisted himself up until his feet slid through the opening.

He landed on the ground in a crouched position, looking left, then right, and listening for anything out of the ordinary. The moon had been eclipsed by a heavy overlay of gray clouds, and he could make out only the outlines of the neighboring buildings. The wind howled through the alleys, carrying the scent of December's heavy monsoons. And something else.

He sniffed twice before he recognized the sour odor of tequila and unwashed bodies.

By then it was too late.

Two men rushed around a nearby corner, tackling him at his knees, while a third wrapped an arm around Will's neck. Black spots flashed in front of his eyes as his oxygen supply diminished.

The men screeched in low tones, ordering each other to hold him down, which Will made relatively simple.

Oh, he maintained the facade of fighting back, clawing at the arm around his neck and kicking one attacker in the stomach. The man grunted and let go. The others just yelled louder. Will let them pull him into a liquor-scented fog and went back to waiting for the right moment.

They didn't know that he had been here before. In this very situation. Without air. Without a weapon.

He'd been trained how to fight back, which made him smile. But only for a second. Then he smashed his head into the face of the man at his back. Cartilage crunched and something hot dripped down Will's neck. The man screamed a string of curses and let go, to cover his broken, bleeding nose.

Taking great gulps of air, Will turned on the man holding his legs. The Panamanian's eyes were wide and vividly white in the darkness, his grip loosening even before Will gave his jaw a solid right hook. The man crumpled into a whimpering heap.

Will spun in a slow circle, glaring down at the attackers littering the ground below his window. They were unorganized and inebriated, and not at all what he'd expect from El Jefe's goons.

And then he knew.

They were just the first wave.

He spun in time to see the outline of a man raise his arm. Will jumped to the side, at the same time a gunshot split the air.

His scalp was on fire. From the root of his hair to the tips, it burned, and something thick and sticky oozed down the side of his face. He tried to lift his head from where it rested against his outstretched arm on the ground, but the flaming pain at his temple kept him firmly in place.

Two men approached him, the one with the gun pointing it again in his direction.

"Wait." Will had never been so happy to hear El Jefe's high-pitched squeak.

"Why?" Even though he could see only feet, Will knew Arturo's slow drawl far too well.

"Because I said so."

Arturo muttered something that Will couldn't

quite make out. Clearly unhappy, he kicked Will in the side, sending him coughing and sputtering in the grass.

Will had been lower than this. He'd been wet and sandy for days. He'd run for miles with a boat over his head. He'd survived Hell Week and the rest of the tortures that filled SEAL training.

A little gunshot wound and a bruised kidney weren't enough to take him out of the picture.

What was it that Luke was always saying? A head wound would bleed forever but rarely kill a man?

Will prayed that was the truth and not just a medic's tall tale, because he had to get to Jess.

He had to get her out of here. He'd promised.

But a promise wasn't enough to keep the darkness from swallowing him whole as Arturo punched him right where the bullet had grazed his skull.

Jess pulled her knees up to her chest, wrapping her arms around her legs and leaning against the unforgiving wall. Her toe tapped an inconsistent beat on the wrench that lay on the floor by her side. Darkness surrounded her, only a sliver of light from the cracks in the door allowing her to distinguish the form of the metal bed frame from the rest of the night.

She'd tried to sleep, but it didn't come easily

after the encounter with Juan Carlos, and Will's cryptic last words to her. *Be ready.*

Of course, it couldn't have anything to do with the heart-stopping kiss he'd given her just before that. Or the way she fit perfectly against his chest. Or the earthy scent of his hair that she still picked up when she closed her eyes.

Resting her chin on her knee, she closed her eyes, just waiting. Waiting for Will.

She'd gotten pretty good at that over the years, but tonight was wrapped up with a red-ribboned promise. He'd sworn that he'd come for her.

And she actually believed he would.

Strange. It hadn't been a conscious decision to put faith in his word again. If it had been, she'd have chosen the other way. She'd have talked herself out of trusting him just to save the inevitable heartache that loving and relying on someone always brought.

Love.

Whoa! Where had that come from?

Will had been closer than a brother, more than just a friend. Ten years ago, she'd cared about him and—if she was truly honest, which this silent cell seemed to demand—she'd loved him with an innocent, childlike love. She'd trusted him, just as she'd trusted her father. Maybe because she saw so many similarities between the two. Strength. Loyalty. Compassion.

Will had tucked her, the new kid, under his arm on their first day of junior high. He'd protected her from the snobby girls and the bullies, and given her a lunch table to join. He'd sat with her on the bus and even walked her most of the way home.

He'd done that, and so much more, for six years. How could she not love him at least a little?

But she most certainly didn't love him now. At all. Even a little bit.

Maybe she'd just keep telling herself that.

At least she could trust him.

He would be there—

A gunshot shattered the silence, and she jumped, cracking her head against a cinder block and letting out a cry. Scrambling to her feet, she scooped up her weapon and sneaked toward the entrance.

The wood was cool and damp as she pressed her ear against the door.

All was silent.

Then came a screech that could have peeled paint.

Lord, please don't let that be Will.

A quiet voice in her heart reminded her that Will would never make a sound like that. He was probably fine. It was likely an out-of-control gambling game. Or someone who had gotten on Juan Carlos's bad side.

Just the thought turned her blood to ice.

She and Will were about to be right there.

Her breath was shaky as she let it out, and she hugged her wrench to her chest. The words of her prayer were lost in the fog of her mind as she fought for control and something stable to cling to as tears streamed unbidden down her cheeks.

"I will never leave you or forsake you."

Nearly audible in the silence, the words of her dad's favorite Bible verse reverberated through every fiber of her being, from the very depths of her soul. She wanted to shout back at the memory of those words.

Her mom had promised the same thing.

Will had said he'd stay by her side.

And where were they now? Her mother had dropped her off at school and never bothered to return for her. And Will? Only God knew if he'd been held up by that firefight. Or worse, involved. Wherever he was, he wasn't where he'd promised to be.

How could she trust that God would be there when no one else in her life seemed capable of sticking around? It was so much easier to believe in a God who came and went on a whim, only as involved as He wanted to be at any given moment.

That was reality. At least that was the reality she knew.

People came and went and there was nothing she could do to keep them with her.

So why did she keep going back to Him, begging for protection and peace in the good times and the bad? And why did He keep showing up when she called?

Hadn't He sent Will when she'd prayed for help? And when she'd asked that Will remain hidden in that closet, whoever had been after them seemed to vanish in the night.

The questions and their more troubling answers swarmed her heart, tearing and clawing at it, until she dropped the wrench from her lifeless fingers. This wasn't the time for her to have this battle. This was the time to escape. She should be over the wall and running for the United States Embassy.

Instead she was glued to the door, waiting for any other sounds of chaos beyond. But there was only silence. And more time with the voice in her mind, the one that reminded her of Sunday school lessons and Bible verses from a safer place.

Here she was, thousands of miles from her home, from everything she knew, and she was still praying. And still, strangely, sure that God heard her. Could it really be that, no matter where she went, He was with her?

Eventually the sun rose, filtering through the cracks in her door. The compound woke up in fits and starts, a low murmur here and there, then nothing for ages. A rumbling jeep and loud shouts, then silence again.

She sank against the wall, slipping all the way to the floor and letting her hands rest in her lap. With her eyes closed the sounds from the compound seemed magnified. Slamming doors and laughter. Marching feet and loud voices.

But they were all faraway. They weren't coming for her.

No one was coming for her.

Especially not Will.

A tear leaked out of her eye. She swiped at it with her fist, gritting her teeth and checking her emotions.

Maybe he'd changed his mind about it being the right time. Maybe he'd forgotten her. Maybe he'd been held up.

By one of Juan Carlos's goons.

Her stomach threatened to jump to her throat as fear raced through her. *Please, God. No.*

Somehow she'd managed to make it through the entire night without letting her mind dwell on the one possibility that was just too much to accept.

If Will had been involved with that gunshot, she was most likely on her own again. It was up to her to make it home in one piece, with the toxin in hand, all by herself.

But could she leave without knowing what had happened to Will?

Jumping to her feet, she snatched the wrench from the floor. She bounced the cool metal in her palm, weighing it against the task at hand, as she eyed the door. The wood was old and splintered and would easily succumb to a few good blows from the tool. But not without drawing the attention of everyone within a hundred yards.

Far too risky.

She ran a finger over the rusted hinges. There were only two of them holding the door in place. Sticking a fingernail into one of the screws securing the brackets, she twisted until her nail broke at the quick. Stopping just short of popping the throbbing digit into her mouth, she surveyed the damage. Just a little blood. And she had far too much to think about to dwell on the pain.

Dropping to her knees, she wedged the wrench beneath the lip of the hinge. Locking her elbows, she put all of her weight onto the tool.

The hinge groaned, and then the wrench slipped free, clattering to the floor.

With a frustrated sigh, Jess picked it back up and tried another angle. It just slipped off again. On the third try she caught her hand on the wrench's teeth, leaving two long, red marks across her palm.

Time had become irrelevant. Only the battle between her and the stubborn hinges mattered.

And finding Will. Making sure he was okay.

She had to make a choice. She could either believe he'd keep his promise if he could or expect him to break it.

She chose to believe.

Two men pushed him forward, and Will stumbled to his knees. His hands, tied behind his back, were of no use, and he landed heavily on his shoulder, squinting against the pain racking every inch of him. His body hurt like it hadn't since Hell Week, or at least since the last time he'd been caught by an enemy sniper's bullet.

Someone shoved his arm and growled at him, but the ringing in his ears blocked out the words.

He wasn't sure he'd ever be able to focus on anything but that buzzing again. But at least he was breathing and conscious. And his heart was still pounding.

Cracking an eye open against the midday sun, he tilted his head back to get a look at his interrogators. Juan Carlos, smug and oily, stood before him, arms crossed and eyes glaring. He was framed by the back door of the big house.

Arturo hung back a step, rubbing his hands together in barely restrained glee. There was another man, but Will couldn't get his left eye open far enough to see if he was a familiar face.

Apparently Arturo had taken the opportunity to work Will over.

Perfect.

"What do you want me to do with him?" Juan Carlos said. "Just get rid of him."

"But he's been sneaking out at night. We caught him crawling out of his window."

As Juan Carlos gave him a cursory glance, Will took quick stock of what was actually injured and what was only bruised. He wiggled digits and limbs as far as he could. Toes and fingers were fine. His legs felt as if they weighed about twice as much as usual. Probably from the blood loss. No problem. He'd run three miles through the sand with a stress fracture in each leg. This was nothing.

Other than a zip tie cutting into his wrists, his left arm was functional. His right elbow stung when he tried to move it. But it moved. It wasn't dislocated or broken.

Good enough.

Juan Carlos waved his hand before resting it on the doorjamb beside him. "Just be done with it. We were never going to keep them around, anyway."

Will's pulse picked up speed. Of course, they had always planned to kill Jess and him, but hearing the edict in such a cold tone sent a chill to his core.

Arturo stepped forward, waving his hands. "What if he knows something?" As he stepped back, the sunlight glinted off a metal blade tucked just inside his boot.

That could come in handy.

Juan Carlos rubbed his temples as if he was the one with the head injury. "Just kill him. Problem solved."

"And the girl?"

"We'll keep her around until we even the score for my brother's murder."

Arturo didn't say anything else. He just grabbed Will's sore elbow, yanked him to his feet and marched toward the front gate, compadre in tow.

They thought he'd been beaten.

Too bad for them, he would do whatever it took to get back to Jess.

THIRTEEN

Jess surveyed her beaten and bruised hands. Swollen fingers. Scraped knuckles. Broken nails.

And all for what? One measly hinge.

The door still wouldn't budge, and she still had to track down Will.

Sudden footsteps pounded toward her door, and she slammed herself back against the wall. Clenching her wrench in both hands, she squeezed her eyes closed, listening. The footsteps stopped right in front of her cell, and the door swung in, popping off its broken hinge.

There was no time to hide her wrench beneath her mattress, so she squatted down to slide it behind the door, hoping the shadows would keep it hidden.

When she stood, Manuel loomed before her, his shoulders broader, his leer more frightening than it ever had been before.

"Vámanos." His command was just as effective as it would have been in English. "We go now."

"The lab?"

He shook his head with a grunt, and she froze. Her feet simply refused to move.

If he took her anywhere but the lab, Will wouldn't know where to find her.

An image of him searching for her and coming up empty-handed flashed across her mind's eye. If he was looking for her—and she had to believe that he was—she had to go someplace he'd search first.

Maybe this was the moment to make a run for it. And if she did, where would Will look for her? *Please, God, let him find me.*

A rush of electricity shot through her legs, and she felt the strength that anxiety and a lack of sleep had stolen from her. She could run.

She had to.

Letting Manuel lock her away wasn't an option. As long as she was free, there was hope. She'd just have to choose her moment very, very carefully.

Taking a cautious step, she followed Manuel into the late-morning sun. The compound buzzed with its usual activities, as though no one recognized that today was the big day. Didn't they realize that everything was about to change?

Manuel pointed his gun down the alley, and she took a deep breath. Walking slowly, she bolstered her courage. Three steps until the cross alley. Two.

One.

She turned left and sprinted as fast as she could.

A split second later her heartbeats drowned out Manuel's screams.

She pumped her arms, working them as hard as she could.

Jess zigzagged between buildings until she lost the sound of Manuel's footsteps, never sparing a glance over her shoulder. But the crack of a gunshot told her that she hadn't lost him yet.

She waited for the sting of a bullet. It didn't come. Only the jarring of her steps over uneven, shifting ground.

Heaving in wet air that tasted like sweat, she fought her way forward, despite every step growing harder.

Her hair stuck to the back of her neck. Her shirt clung to her damp back.

Still the only sound in her ears was the steady *thump-thump* of her heart.

Alleys became a confusing maze as she turned and dashed from one to another. Finally she broke free into the narrow lane along the outer wall.

The crack of a gun butt slamming into her chest startled her before she realized she'd been hit. It actually took a second for the pain to kick in.

And then all of her air was gone and she tumbled forward, clawing at the mud.

By the time Will had marched through the gate, past the northwest corner guard tower and so far off the beaten path that Arturo probably figured Will would never be able to trace his steps back, his pant legs were caked with mud up to his knees. Still, Arturo pushed him forward, toward the jungle.

Arturo's friend muttered under his breath, "Do we have to go farther? Why can't we just do it here?"

Will recognized that voice. He sneaked a peek at the face of the man who had lost the bet with Arturo on whether Will was in his room. Raul's eyes were too big for his face, his hairline receding, although he didn't look much beyond thirty.

"Did you bring a shovel, Raul?" Arturo grabbed Will's arm and yanked on it. Will faked a stumble, tripping into Raul, who nearly toppled at the contact. Suspicion confirmed; when the time was right, Raul would go down without much of a fight.

"No."

"Then we take him into the jungle where he won't stink up the kitchen."

Raul grumbled under his breath. "This is worse than when we planted the land mines."

So the red marks on the map were mines, and he was going to have to find his way through them. He pictured the map, visualizing their locations and the best place to get back inside the compound.

But first, Will was going to fight. And he wasn't going to lose this one. He wasn't who they thought he was. He was a United States Navy SEAL.

And there was no way he would let two thugs keep him from finding Jess.

The jungle wall seemed to have been cut clean from top to bottom by a machete. The canopy rose straight out of the ground, leaving an ideal clearing for the less impressive security wall behind them.

When they finally reached the wall of green, Raul put a shaking hand on Will's shoulder.

"Get down."

Will held his ground, wiggling his wrists again, stretching the plastic.

"Stupid American." Arturo cursed in Spanish and spit next to Will's foot. He clearly thought he hadn't understood. "Down."

"I heard you," Will said in Spanish. His voice surprised even himself, it was so low and lethal.

He tried to school his emotions, channel all his training into a response to this single moment.

His heartbeat drowned out every sound of the

jungle. The mumbling of his guards faded. His fists pulled tight.

This was why he'd spent years in the world's most intense training, building the skills so that he'd be able to protect those who could not protect themselves. Whether or not he'd known them for sixteen years.

Jess's face flashed across the back of his eyelids.

Suddenly the pain that had clamped on his temple released, and a smile spread across his face.

Arturo had no idea what was coming.

"Then get down on the ground." The Panamanian's words were thick and angry, and Will didn't have to see his face to know he was sneering. Arturo raised his pistol. It was old and corroded, but it still worked. Will had firsthand knowledge of that. And at three feet, even the brute couldn't miss his mark.

With a silent prayer for speed, accuracy and Jess's safety, Will dropped to one knee. He jerked his other leg out, fast and hard.

Raul squealed like a pig as his leg buckled, and he hit the ground with another cry of pain.

Arturo stood frozen, his eyes wide and his mouth hanging open. The weapon in his hand dangled dangerously.

Will jumped to his feet and charged the stunned man. His shoulder connected with Arturo's stomach, knocking the wind out of him as they tumbled to the earth. The Panamanian's fingers poked at Will's face, and he instinctively jerked his head away from the threat of more pain. With a well-placed knee, he elicited a shriek of agony before diving for the blade he'd seen hidden inside Arturo's boot.

He wedged it between the heels of his hands and the plastic zip tie, and sliced his bindings.

Rotating his shoulders was like a gift from above, and he sent a quick thanks in that direction.

Just as Will freed himself, Raul hobbled back toward them, heavily favoring his leg. He lunged for the dropped gun, but Will was faster. With a quick punch to the guard's windpipe, he sent him to the ground.

Using their belts and shoelaces, he secured their hands and feet to keep them from running for help. At this distance from the compound, he wasn't worried about anyone hearing them calling, either. Before he left them, he pulled off Arturo's jacket and hat. A little camouflage could go a long way in the middle of chaos. And Will had a distinct feeling that chaos was about to become the norm.

Only the shallow rise and fall of their chests and occasional groans confirmed that Arturo and Raul were still alive as Will rolled them beyond the tree line. Leaving them, he turned back in the direction of the compound. He needed to get to Jess. She would think he'd left her again, and he couldn't stomach the thought.

But if he was going to reach her, he had to think through his approach. If he retraced the route they'd taken to the jungle wall, he'd arrive at the front gate and be greeted by guards toting machine guns.

But the only other way inside those walls was across a minefield and over a barbed-wire fence.

Will rubbed the abrasions on his wrists, pondering his options. A muddy path to a violent confrontation or a surprise attack.

Juan Carlos would start to ask questions when Arturo didn't return, so Will couldn't stand around for long, trying to make a decision.

There was no question.

He had to go over the wall. But first he had to clear a trail.

Whipping his head back and forth, he hunted for a tool, but found nothing. There had to be something that would apply enough pressure to a land mine to detonate it, but would allow him to stay at least fifty feet back to avoid more injuries.

He dropped his chin to his chest, pinched his eyes closed and said, "God, I need help."

When he opened his eyes, he caught a glimpse of a moss-covered log to his left.

"Thank You."

He jogged over to the answer to his prayer, squatted down and rocked the wooden beam free of its resting place. With another push, it rolled forward, and he shoved it again and again until it reached the top of a low hill almost fifty yards from the compound wall. Taking one long breath and then holding it, he gave another push.

The log barreled down the hill, bumping but not bouncing as it picked up speed. Time stood still as it reached a third of the way to the wall. Nothing happened.

Will pinched the bridge of his nose and exhaled.

Maybe it wouldn't work. Maybe he'd misjudged the weight of the log or the pressure required to set off a land mine. Maybe he'd remembered the mine placement wrong. Maybe—

The explosion nearly blinded him, and he threw up his arms to block the shower of grass and earth that rained down.

He'd taken one step in the log's cleared path when another mine exploded. And another.

Ears ringing, he chased the wooden sweeper down the hill. He was careful to keep just enough distance from it in case it found another hidden target.

And then the log crashed into the security wall, setting off a fourth explosion. By now, Will could hear the response from inside the compound. The shouts and ruckus were nearly as loud as the mines themselves.

He ran straight toward the melee. Pushing off what little remained of the log, he launched himself up the wall, his feet scrabbling to find purchase as his fingers clenched the top. His muscles strained to pull him up, the feeling of weakness throughout his body strange and probably a side effect of his head wound.

With a grunt and a sigh, he reached the rim. A knee held him in place as he flung Arturo's jacket across the barbed wire and scrambled over it. A shard of glass caught his hand, but Will barely noticed the blood dripping down his fingers.

He just had to find Jess.

It was dark when Jess came to.

Well, not quite. Bright light fought through the heavy curtains shrouding the windows as she crawled to her knees on a plush Oriental rug, but the room itself was dim. Her arms and legs shook under her own weight, her chest burning.

Pressing a hand over her sternum, she winced. Memories flooded back.

Manuel had caught her and stopped her with a gun to her chest. She'd crumpled like wet paper. And she felt just about as strong.

"Well, well. Look who's finally decided to join us."

She jerked her head in the direction of the silky voice. She could see only his legs, one ankle crossed over a bent knee, as he rested in a leather wingback chair. His face was hidden in shadow, but she knew it was Juan Carlos.

"What do you want with me?" Her words came out with a cough and a wheeze. But she locked her elbows rather than give in to the lure of resting on the carpet.

"I just want you to do your job. And then I want you to go away."

Permanently.

It was never spoken, but she still heard it, louder than a cargo train.

"I'm not going to release the Morsyni."

He laughed with all the panache of a cartoon villain twirling his mustache. "Of course you are."

"No. I'm not." As she said the words, she knew they were true. She was the only person in this compound capable of transferring the toxin into the dispenser without killing everyone within a half-mile radius. If she refused to help, it would kill only those who meant to use it against their enemies. And Will. And her.

But if she couldn't escape with it, she could

at least make sure that no one outside the compound was injured.

"I won't let you use it against people who don't deserve it."

"You think they're innocent?" Juan Carlos jumped to his feet, pacing right in front of her.

She didn't have the strength to look up, so she let her head hang low as she sucked in another breath. A cool, dry breath.

She was somewhere with an air conditioner. The temperature in the room was actually cool enough to dry her sweat into itchy salt. Ignoring the urge to scratch, she savored the cool air and tried to focus on a way out. They must have taken her to the big house. Which meant she was right next to the shed. If she could get on top of that, maybe she could get over the fence.

Without Will.

If she was certain that he hadn't left her—and she was—then she couldn't do it to him, either. She had to stall long enough for Will to find her. Long enough for her to come up with an escape route for them both.

The thought nearly made her laugh. Will needed her help about as much as he needed a compass without a needle. He hadn't come down here because he couldn't handle the cartel. He'd come because *she* couldn't handle them. Because he cared about her.

Because sometimes people came back.

Juan Carlos was still pacing like a cheetah, infinitely groomed, yet feral. He growled low in his throat, mumbling something over and over to himself. Finally he exploded. "Answer me. You think they're innocent? You think killing my brother was an innocent act?"

Her muscles twitched. "No."

"He was a good man. A good brother. And he was studying in America."

Jess tamped down the fear that threatened to choke her. She knew something about school. Maybe she could keep Juan Carlos talking, distract him from whatever he had planned for her. "What was he studying?"

"Medicine."

Oh, the irony. One brother learning to heal, the other intent on destruction. "How far did he get in his studies?"

Juan Carlos's feet stopped off to her right, pointing toward the unlit fireplace. He was quiet for a long moment. Maybe he hadn't heard her. More likely he was tired of answering her questions.

"He was just about to finish medical school. My father left Los Verdes—" that must be the name of the cartel "—to the both of us, but Pedro insisted on finishing his education." Emotion tugged at the cold man's words, and Jess wanted to understand the love of a brother strong enough to kill for. But it just made her cold all over.

Will hadn't killed for his brother. Instead, he'd sacrificed his entire life in San Diego to protect Sal—but from what? From her?

"He was only here for a visit." Juan Carlos's gravelly voice jerked her from her memories of the other brothers. "But the raiders came in the middle of the night. Greedy and hungry for blood. They wanted my land and my money, so they blew up a corner of the fence. Pedro ran outside and was cut down by a machine gun."

The drug lord squatted in front of her. His hand slithered into her hair, and she tried to shake off the shivers that accompanied his touch. Strong fingers fisted against her scalp, and he yanked her head up to gaze into his eyes, which were like ice.

"He was twenty-five. Just a young man, with so much left to do." Juan Carlos's grip on her hair tightened, and she let out an involuntary wince. His lips twisted in a wicked smile, making it clear he took pleasure in her pain. "They are not innocent. And they're going to pay. And you're going to help me make them."

She shook her head as much as his grasp allowed, fighting down the panic that was rising in her chest.

"No. I won't kill anyone."

He flung her head to the side, the force toppling

her to the carpet. She rubbed her aching shoulders and took three shaky breaths. The room smelled of lemon furniture polish and too much cologne. And captivity.

"If you won't help, then you're of no use to me." He swooped down on her, grabbing her by the arm and hauling her to her feet before dragging her to the hall.

She flailed and kicked at him, but her feet seemed to strike the narrow walls more than flesh.

Jess screamed and yelled, hoping to draw the attention of Sergio, who had always been more kind than her own guard. But maybe even Manuel, with his angry leer, wouldn't watch her be led to her death. She just had to catch someone's attention.

Suddenly an explosion shook the walls of the house.

It was too much to hope that Juan Carlos would forget her in the commotion. Instead he dug his hand deeper into the meat of her arm, marching with more purpose toward the door at the end of the hall.

Just as he threw her into the yard at the back of the big house, three loud bangs sounded in quick succession. Clumps of mud and dirt shot over the top of the fence, and Juan Carlos swore loudly in more languages than she could count.

Men poured out of barracks like ants out of a flooded hill. Guns held tight, some charged for the front gate. Others ran in the direction of the explosions. Everyone yelled at the same time, drowning other voices out in the din.

Including her own.

Jess screamed as she lurched to her feet, hoping to remain invisible amid the chaos. But then Juan Carlos was back, his breath hot and sticky on her neck as he hauled her against his chest. His laughter rang in her ears, and all she could do was scratch at the arm wrapped around her. "Let me go! I have to find Will. Where is he?"

"Oh, he's long dead by now."

Terror clawed at her insides. The certainty behind his words left her frozen in place.

Dear God, he can't be gone. Please, don't let him be gone.

She hadn't forgiven Will yet. At least she hadn't told him that she'd forgiven him. And she needed to.

She *wanted* to.

And now she'd never have a chance to hold him again, to wrap her arms around his waist. To kiss him.

Tears streaked down her cheeks as Juan Carlos dug sharp fingernails into her skin.

She cried, not for herself, but for the man she

had loved, the one who had stayed in her heart for ten years.

Now she'd lost him.

Forever.

A sob escaped her throat as Juan Carlos pushed her to the ground. From the back of his waistband, he produced a long, lethal handgun and leveled it at her head.

"You've been more trouble than you're worth."

She squeezed her eyes shut, pressed her fists to her mouth and waited for the last sound she'd ever hear.

FOURTEEN

Will landed within the compound walls, his knees bending low to cushion the fall. His gaze darted up and down the alleyway. It was still deserted save for the shouts of men—some rushing toward him, others away.

The explosions had served to not only clear his path but also distract anyone who would try to stop him from completing his mission. He just needed to distance himself from the scene of the explosions as fast as he could. He sprinted in the direction of Jess's room, but a piercing scream stopped him in his tracks.

He knew that voice, and the fear in it sent tremors through his entire body.

Holding his breath, he waited, praying he'd hear it again so he'd know which way to go.

Jess's second scream launched him toward the big house.

As he turned a corner, he nearly slammed into a surprised field hand. Without more than a glance, Will shoved the man to the ground and kept running.

His hands shook, so he drew them into tight fists, pushing his feet faster. With his pulse pounding in his ears, he forced himself beyond what he'd even thought possible.

Lord, please let me be in time.

He had to find her. Had to save her.

Because even if he couldn't be with her, he had to know that she was out there. That her smile was still contagious and her laughter was still filling a room. Somewhere.

Rounding the back of the big house, he caught sight of Jess kneeling on the ground. Juan Carlos held a gun leveled at her head.

Will saw only the weapon. He lunged for it.

It fired with a crack, and everything inside Will burst forth. He wrestled with Juan Carlos, who punched his head. It didn't slow him down. The adrenaline wiped out any pain from his injuries. Grabbing the kingpin by the shirt, Will slammed him to the grass and pressed his knee into his chest. Fear-filled eyes bugged out, and Will just pushed harder. The other man's mouth moved, but Will couldn't hear anything beyond the thudding of his own heart.

He popped Juan Carlos with a right jab to the chin, which knocked him out cold.

Will immediately looked around for Jess, who

lay on the ground, her arms and legs splayed. A dark stain marred her light blue shirt.

Had she been hit by the bullet? His throat closed and his heart stopped.

The entire world ceased spinning as he crawled to her, pressing a hand to the sticky mess at her side. If he could put enough pressure on the wound, he could keep her alive. He just had to keep her alive.

Her lashes fluttered, finally revealing clear eyes filled with…he couldn't quite put his finger on the emotion there. Remorse, maybe. But not pain.

"Are you hit?"

She shook her head. "I don't think so."

Lifting his hands, he inspected the mud caked there. The only blood on his fingers was his own. The stain on her shirt, and now on his hands, was mostly just the grimy remnants of the December rains she'd rolled in.

Relief washed over him, and he was able to breathe again. He sat back on his heels, cradling her in his arms and holding her tight against his chest. Pressing his nose to her hair, he inhaled her warmth. Her living, breathing warmth.

"I thought I'd lost you there for a second."

She wrapped an arm around his middle and snuggled into his embrace. Her hands roved over his arms and shoulders. "You're alive."

"You sound surprised." He leaned away enough to get a good look into her face and to catch a stilted nod and pinched eyes.

"Yes. No. Juan Carlos said you were dead, and I thought—I thought I would never see you again. I thought I'd never get to tell you…" She dived back into Will's arms, a damp pool of heat spreading across his shirt.

Rubbing gentle circles on her back, he whispered words of comfort. Nonsense that he hoped she understood, because he had only an inkling of what it really meant.

Actually, that wasn't entirely true. He knew what he was saying, if not in so many words.

I love you.

He just wasn't free to tell her that.

And this was the last time he'd get to hold her like this, heart to heart. His pulse matched her tempo, speeding up with every tremble of her shoulders, every silent sob. She fit against him as if she'd been made just for his arms, just for his love.

Pressing his lips to the top of her head, he whispered, "We're okay. And we're going to go home."

She didn't look up, and he almost missed her response. "Together?"

If only he could tell her yes.

His pulse quickly outpaced hers, until all he could hear was every individual beat of his heart.

Then the beat grew louder, a thunder that no longer came from inside him. It whirled around them, the wind pressing them to the ground. He didn't even need to look over his shoulder at the giant green beast to recognize the distinctive sound of a Chinook.

The cavalry had arrived.

Even as a beautiful black woman in a blue DEA jacket and a tall man in battle dress uniform ran toward them, Jess didn't loosen her grip on Will. He tried to lean away, but she'd latched on so tightly that she just moved with him.

"Willie G!"

Responding to the call, Will scooped her up and ran toward the two new arrivals. Behind them were even more men in camouflage, herding confused cartel guards into the courtyard.

"Cubby!" Will's greeting made the tall sailor's ears turn pink, but he clapped Will on the shoulder with enough force to topple a smaller man. "Are you hurt, ma'am?"

It took Jess several seconds to realize that the man was speaking to her. She tried to respond, but her tongue refused to obey.

Before she could get anything out, Will answered for her. "Let's get her checked out, just to be safe."

"No." The single word took a ridiculous amount

of effort. "I'm fine." Just shaken. And scared. And completely unsure what exactly was going on.

But it was too late to argue. Already the man called Cubby—who looked far too broad to have acquired such a cute nickname—was running sure but gentle fingers down her arms and legs. He cupped her neck and prodded the back of her scalp, which sent shards of pain around her head. She winced and pulled away.

"Did that hurt, ma'am?"

"Jess." She sighed and burrowed into Will's shoulder. If only she could just stay there forever. Then the pain at the base of her skull would subside, and she'd always be cared for. Always protected.

Always with the man she loved.

The grade-school-teacher look on Cubby's face broke, a smile full of straight, white teeth taking its place. "Yes, ma'am—Jess."

The DEA agent came to join them. "How about you, Willie? That gash on your head looks pretty nasty."

Will's chuckle vibrated Jess's shoulder. "You'll notice that Cub didn't bother looking to see if I was injured first. Straight for the girl. Every time."

Will began walking again, making no motion

to set her down, which was just fine with Jess. She wasn't sure her legs would carry her, anyway.

"Hey, I figured you'd take care of yourself. You never let me look at your stuff, anyway."

"Maybe I'll let you stitch me up this time. It's been bleeding all day."

Cubby chuckled and nodded as they reached the chopper and Will stepped on board. Squatting, he lowered Jess to a bench seat along the wall.

The radio on the agent's belt squawked, and she picked up it up and mumbled something into it. "Backup is on the way. We'll be out of here soon."

"Wait." Jess pulled herself away from the wall, her head still spinning. "The toxin. It's still in the lab."

"We'll get it."

"Don't open the container."

The agent nodded, hurried outside and ordered someone to retrieve the deadly package.

Will sat down next to Jess, his hand resting on hers as Cub knelt in front of him. Opening a white medical kit, the tall man swabbed at the blood oozing over Will's ear.

"I didn't expect to see you here." Will flinched, and Cub laughed.

"You're a bad liar." He dug back into his supplies. "You knew I'd be here. It's what best friends do."

Jess's heart skipped a beat. So this was Luke. Will's new best friend.

Will's gaze swung to meet hers, and there was something akin to an apology in his eyes. He'd said the words over and over, but apparently he felt the need to express them again.

"McCoy was getting itchy for some word, so I talked him into letting me join the DEA team tracking your GPS."

"How'd you know the XO sent me down here?"

Luke shrugged and tipped his head in the direction of the agent who had just left. "Amy told me you asked her to get you kidnapped by some drug cartel. That's pretty crazy, even for you. I figured something was up. You'd never take off without a good reason."

Will squeezed Jess's fingers, and her stomach lurched. She yanked her hand into her lap, away from his warmth and any reminder that she suddenly didn't fit in, as the men bantered.

"Meet the XO's daughter."

Luke's expression would have been funny under any other circumstance. His Adam's apple bobbed, and he blinked four times, his gaze bouncing between her and Will. For a moment it looked as if he was going to jump to his feet and salute. Thankfully, he stayed on his knees. "Petty Officer Second Class Luke Dunham, ma'am."

She nodded. "Jess McCoy. Nice to meet you."

The next thirteen hours passed in a blur, and Jess remembered only bits and pieces of them.

DEA agent Amy Delgado had returned to the chopper carrying the sealed black box that contained the Morsyni powder. Shortly after, two smaller choppers had arrived with backup, although Juan Carlos, El Jefe and the other henchmen had long since been detained. The new arrivals swept the jungle at Will's suggestion and found Arturo and Raul still struggling to get free.

Amy had to stay on the ground, cleaning up the mess, working with the local authorities and identifying who could be prosecuted for international crimes.

As she hopped out of the chopper's cargo bay, she waved. "There's a military transport headed from the U.S. Embassy in about an hour. They've saved you three a spot on it."

"Thank you, Amy." Will shook her hand. "Your timing was great. I'm glad you found us."

She nodded. "It was a close one. We couldn't narrow in on you because the jungle is so dense in this area. The cell towers are miles away, and we never would have located you if you hadn't set off those explosions."

Will just shrugged, as if it was all part of a day's work. And for him, it probably was.

"There's an office at the front of the admin

building next to the big house. The desk along the north wall is packed with ledgers, and I think I saw a flight book in there. It might help you make your case."

She smiled, gave a thumbs-up and ran off just as the helicopter rotors began their rhythmic thumping.

It was too loud in the bay of the chopper to talk, so Jess settled between Will and Luke and leaned her pounding head against the mesh netting over her seat. Before she knew it they were on the transport plane headed for San Diego.

As Will buckled himself into a jump seat, he finally smiled. Although streaks of dark red still clung to his hair, his face was mostly clean thanks to Luke's handiwork. "Looks like you're going to make it home in time for Christmas," Will said.

Right. Christmas.

It had seemed so important just a few days before. Jess had longed to be home to celebrate with her dad.

But now she realized that meant watching Will walk away, and she just wasn't sure she could survive that again.

Whether it was Luke's presence or the crashing adrenaline, they didn't speak during the seven-hour flight home. Jess sat and stared at her folded hands, wondering how she was going to manage to say goodbye. After a few hours, she sneaked a peek at Will, who sat with his head back, eyes closed. His shoulders rose and fell in the slow tempo of a man finally able to rest.

He was so handsome, even with a smear of mud from his chin to the corner of his eye. So peaceful now. So secure.

She was safe with him. He'd rescued her, just as he'd said he would.

But he hadn't made her any promises beyond Panama.

Somehow it didn't stop her heart from aching for a future that he didn't want. One where he never took off.

It was Luke who finally broke the silence. Sitting on her other side, he leaned in, raising his voice just enough to be heard over the humming engines of the massive cargo plane. "He talks about you a lot."

Her head spun toward the baby-faced SEAL. "He does?"

"It's always, 'Jess did this. Jess used to do that.'" He nudged her elbow with his own and grinned. "I always wondered what kind of girl could stick with a bum like that for so long."

Her neck burned, and she pressed a hand to her throat. "He said you taught him how to pick a lock."

"Of course. Of all the things we've done, that's

the one he tells everyone about. Makes me sound like a two-bit thief."

"No. Not at all. He just—he said it helps you relax."

A corner of Luke's mouth pulled to the side as his forehead wrinkled. "I suppose. We all have our own ways of dealing with the stress of the job. Some of the guys play video games. Some work out all the time. I guess I like some time with just me and a lock."

"What's Will's?" As soon as the words were out, she wished she could take them back. She shouldn't have asked. She didn't need to know.

But mostly she wished she already knew.

"Will?" Luke grunted. "Mostly he just talks about family dinners and his grandma's enchiladas. And after a particularly rough mission, he'll talk about this cute brunette who used to sit next to him at the table and talk him into midnight swimming."

Her face blazed, and she had to look back at her knees. Butterflies swarmed in her stomach, but she refused to be their victim. Just because Will remembered her, talked about her, didn't change anything.

"You know, he was the one who always suggested swimming after my curfew."

Luke chuckled.

The plane lurched, its nose diving. She gasped, her fist clenching her grimy pants.

Suddenly Will's hand found hers, and he twined their fingers together, letting her squeeze as they continued their descent.

She risked a glance at Will, whose eyes were still closed, then at Luke, who gave her a saucy wink.

"I guess they don't tell you to put your tray tables up on cargo flights."

"And I don't think I ever got my peanuts," Will said, his eyes fluttering open.

Jess didn't have time to wonder how much of their conversation he had heard. Soon the wheels bounced on the runway, and they were tossed around within the confines of their seat belts. When the bay doors opened, the plane was flooded with light from the setting sun and with the sweet smell of salt water.

Jess's legs trembled as she stood, but she ran, anyway. Though no one had told her to expect him, she knew her dad would be waiting for her. As she cleared the ramp, he was there in his white dress uniform, arms spread wide.

She'd never hugged anyone as tightly, while he kissed her cheeks and ran his hands over her hair. Tears streamed down his face, and he mumbled something that she couldn't hear over the war raging in her heart.

How could a moment be at once so sweet and so heartbreaking?

"I was so worried about you," he said against her temple. "I'm so glad you're home."

"Me, too, Dad."

After what felt like hours, her dad stepped back, finally taking notice of the two shadows standing off to his left.

"Gumble. Dunham."

Both men snapped to attention at his deep voice, tension rolling off them.

A smile cracked her dad's demeanor. "Good work, men. Thank you for bringing her back to me."

Will stepped forward to shake his hand. "My pleasure, sir." Luke quickly followed suit and then stepped back.

"I suppose you two are due a little leave."

"No, sir," Will said.

The XO's forehead wrinkled. "Eager to get back to your team?"

Will nodded, his hands clasped behind his back. "Yes, sir."

"All right, then. I'll let Lieutenant Sawyer know to expect you back tomorrow."

"Thank you." Will took a step back, as though he was going to excuse himself. He squinted into the last sliver of orange sun still visible over the horizon.

A rope squeezed Jess's chest, and she stumbled toward him, her hand outstretched. He caught it and pulled her into his embrace in one smooth movement.

"I hope you have a merry Christmas." He dipped his head to kiss her cheek, his lips leaving a mark so strong that it had to be visible. "When we were down there…you did really good, kid."

Oh, there was too much she needed to say. And no privacy in which to say it. Her brain froze, and she could only hold on to him.

He gave her a quick squeeze. Then, just like ten years before, he let her go and walked out of her life.

At least this time he said goodbye.

But it would never be enough.

FIFTEEN

Will paced the steps in front of his brother's office building more times than he could count. He'd held open the door for five different women walking up to the glass doors. Still he couldn't get up the nerve to go in there and talk to Sal face-to-face.

Luke, L.T. and Rock had all told him that if he didn't pull himself out of his funk, they were going to send him back to Panama.

If Jess had still been there, he'd have gladly gone.

But she wasn't. She was about fifteen miles away, which might as well have been in another hemisphere.

He scrubbed his hands over his face and stared at the perfect blue sky. Why did this have to be so hard? He should just be able to go into that office and tell his brother the truth. Except he owed Sal more than he could repay. Sal deserved better than a brother like Will. Sal deserved a brother who wasn't falling deeper and deeper for the girl Sal still loved.

"Will?"

He jumped at the sound of his name.

Sal walked up the steps from the parking garage, black tubes tucked under his arm. "What are you doing here?"

He ran a hand through his hair and shrugged.

Sal smiled widely, a match of Will's own dimple appearing in his right cheek. "Come on inside." He held open the door for Will, then led the way through a maze of cubicles into an office in the back corner.

Will had been in this office a handful of times, and nothing had changed. An architect's drawing table sat in a corner opposite a giant wooden desk. Three black trays stacked on the corner contained the only visible paper.

Will gestured toward the clock on the wall next to a row of framed diplomas. "Getting in kind of late today, eh?"

Sal laughed. "I was showing a client some new designs for her renovation this morning." He set down his blueprint tubes before settling into the leather chair behind the desk. "Why don't you sit down? Tell me how you're doing."

Eyeing the plush chairs facing the desk, Will shook his head. Instead he paced the length of the room and back, clawing at his scalp and praying for a flash of brilliance.

"Man, something's under your skin." Sal leaned forward, his elbows on his desk. "It can't be that bad. Mom called me this morning, and she didn't say anything was wrong. Just spit it out."

Will stopped long enough to stare into his brother's eyes, but quickly resumed his pacing. Motion usually helped him think. But apparently not today.

"Listen. See…here's the thing…" He shook his head and started over. "You kept me from being sent to military school."

"What? Where did that come from?" Sal settled back into his chair. "That was years ago."

"I know, but you didn't have to spend that night in jail. You could have let Dad send me off to Texas."

Sal shook his head. "I don't understand. What is this all about?"

"I—I owe you. A lot."

"We're brothers. We don't keep score."

That stopped Will in his tracks. If what Sal said was true, then maybe there was hope yet. Maybe he would understand.

Will had never been so terrified in his life. His entire future rested on his next words and his brother's response. "I'm in love with Jess."

Sal's eyes narrowed, and he pressed his palms against his desk. "Jess? McCoy?"

"Yes."

Sal waved two fingers between them. "This is all about you being in love with Jess?"

"I'm sorry, man. I know how you feel—"

Laughter filled the air, and Will jerked to a halt midstride.

"I know you're in love with Jess," Sal said, his voice laced with amusement. "Do you think I'm stupid?"

Will collapsed into a chair, pressing a hand over his flopping stomach. "But I thought you were still in love with her."

"Even I knew I was a fool for asking her to marry me. You two only had eyes for each other, even back then."

A battering ram slammed into Will's chest, and he leaned over his knees to catch his breath.

Sal laughed again. "You thought I've been pining over her all these years?"

"But you haven't settled down or even really dated much. I just figured…"

"Architecture school and starting my own firm took all of my time. When would I have fit a serious relationship into that?"

"So you're not…you're okay with me and Jess?"

Sal walked around his desk and slapped Will's shoulder. "Of course I am. You two are made for each other. I just can't believe it's taken you so long to realize it."

Will jumped from his seat. He hadn't even felt so light when the Chinook arrived in Panama.

Pulling Sal into a bear hug, he said, "Thank you." Then he raced for the exit.

"Where are you going?"

He skidded to a stop at the door just long enough to holler over his shoulder. "To tell Jess how I feel."

Jess sat behind the wheel of her coupe, staring at the sprawling blue house across the street. She'd intended to go back to her job at the lab this morning, but somehow she'd ended up in front of Pacific Coast House, a safe haven for those who had suffered at the hands of domestic violence.

She'd been volunteering there for a little over a year and knew how secure the facility was. How the safety there allowed mothers and children to flourish.

And right that moment, she needed a haven where she could feel safe.

She slammed her car door behind her, jogged across the street and opened the white door, which boasted a small welcome sign.

Dawn, the receptionist, looked up from her computer at the front desk. "Jess! I didn't think we'd see you this week. Staci said you were out of town."

Jess managed a half smile. "Just got back a couple days ago. Thought I'd see if there's anything I could do to help out around here."

"Oh, always." Dawn waved her hands as though the whole house might fall down under a strong breeze. "Ashley's in the kitchen with Jasper. I'm sure she could use a hand."

Jess practically ran down the hallway toward the wide kitchen, which featured bright white cupboards and cheery yellow curtains. As she turned the corner, the top of Ashley's blond ponytail peeked over the open fridge door. Seconds later, a toddler with wild blond curls ran up to Jess, his arms outstretched as he danced on his tippy toes. "Up. Up."

Jess laughed and scooped Jasper into her arms, giving him a quick spin for good measure.

"Oh, you don't have to carry him." Ashley emerged from the fridge, her arms full of vegetables that nearly covered her swelling belly.

"I don't mind a bit." Jess tickled the squirming boy, and his laughter was like a healing balm to her aching heart. "You probably can't hold him much anymore."

With a knowing roll of her eyes, Ashley rubbed the small of her back. "I didn't think it was possible to be more uncomfortable than I was when I was pregnant with Jasper, but this little one feels like he's taking up twice as much room, and I still have another month to go."

"Well, his dad isn't exactly petite."

Ashley laughed. "He most certainly is not."

Jasper was heavier than he looked, so Jess pulled a chair out from the table, sat down and started bouncing him on her knees. He squealed with glee, which earned a smile from his mom before she turned back to chopping veggies.

"We didn't expect you this week," Ashley said after a long silence.

Before she could respond, quick footsteps in the hallway announced a new arrival, and Staci Sawyer swung through the door frame, panting for breath, her cheeks pink. "You're back!"

"I know, I know." Jess's smile felt too forced. "You didn't expect me this week."

Staci knelt to give her an awkward hug and plant a kiss on her nephew's cheek. He immediately held out his arms and leaned into Staci. Jess gave him up with one last brush of her fingers through his silky curls.

With her hands empty, she joined Ashley at the counter, longing for something to do. Anything that would take her mind off of Will's renewed absence. Peeling carrots didn't fill the void, but it helped to pass the time.

"So?" Staci's voice was low as she closed the

partition to the dining room. "Are you going to tell us about it?"

"Tell you about what?"

Ashley quirked her lips to the side, shooting Jess a look that said she wasn't fooling anyone.

Jess stared at her carrots as though they were the most interesting orange food ever created, but she couldn't find any words to explain what had happened, what it had been like. She didn't even know how much they knew. Their husbands did work with Will, so her friends had probably heard more than she'd told a soul, even her dad.

"Tristan says that Willie has been—how do I put this nicely?—a bear since he got back." Staci plopped Jasper on the counter so she could stand right next to Jess. "What happened?"

"Nothing." Oh, there had never been a bigger lie, and her friends' eyes told her they knew it. "Everything," Jess said with a sigh.

Ashley and Staci shared a knowing look. "We both know a thing about that," Ashley said. "Spill it."

Before she could stop, Jess let it all out. The kidnapping. Waking up in Panama. Seeing Will again. All their history.

She told them about everything but the kisses. Those were hers alone to remember. And when she needed a smile, she pulled out the memory of being in his arms. Of feeling wholly, incomparably cherished. And for a moment she was with him again.

Until reality interrupted, leaving that aching void in her chest that kept her awake at night.

"For ten years I held on to this thread of hope that someday Will would come back to me. But when he did, he left again. And this time it's forever. Just like my mom." Jess sniffed, the carrots swimming before her suddenly watery eyes.

"Oh, honey." Staci rubbed Jess's back. "What does your dad say?"

"He says I need to let go of the past, to forgive my mom for leaving." Jess wiped her eyes with the back of her hand before attacking another carrot with the peeler. "He also says Will isn't like her, that he's a good man."

"Your dad sounds like a smart guy."

Jess swallowed a hiccup. "I know he's right, and I'm trying really hard not to make this about my mom. But Will did walk away. Again."

"It's hard to be with a SEAL," Ashley said, as she washed several stalks of celery. "You never know when they'll be called up or how long the next deployment will last."

"Yes, but you at least know that they want to come home to you, right?"

Staci nodded slowly.

"Will had his chance. He looked me in the eye on that tarmac, gave me a hug and took off."

Jasper, apparently sensing the tension in the room, leaned forward and hugged Jess around the neck. She patted his back and kissed his forehead. "My mom didn't want me. And I've dealt with that. But even though my dad was deployed all the time, I knew he *wanted* to come home. Will doesn't want any kind of relationship with me."

"Did you ask him if that's really how he feels?" Staci asked.

"I couldn't risk it."

Ashley's eyes narrowed. "Why not go tell him how you feel?"

"I can't chase him down." She arranged her carrot sticks into neat rows, wishing that it was as easy to give some order to her out-of-control emotions. "I'd never know when he was going to leave, but I'd always be waiting for him to."

Staring at her hands, Ashley asked the question that had to be answered. "But if he did—if he came back now—could you forgive him?"

Jess knuckled away the tears that leaked down her cheeks as everything inside of her constricted. "I already have."

She was still mopping up her running mascara when the door swung open. Dawn poked her head in, her eyebrows scrunched together. "Jess, there's someone here to see you."

"Me?" Her stomach jumped, then took a dive. She had no reason to hope it could be Will.

"I sent him into the living room, since lunch will be happening in here soon."

Him.

It couldn't be. It wasn't. She couldn't let herself even wish.

Wiping her hands on a towel, she took a shaky breath and followed Dawn down the hall.

Will leaned a hand against the white mantel decked out in garlands and red stockings. Miniature versions of the classic socks hung on the broad tree in the corner, and its white lights danced on the far wall. Several large boxes below the branches were wrapped in blue and green paper, and he stuck his hand in his pocket, fingering the gift there.

It was corny and ridiculous.

And maybe it would be enough to tell her how he really felt.

He had never been great with words.

Please, God, just give me the words to say today. Help her forgive me—maybe even love me.

He sensed more than heard her arrival, and he spun to face her. Jess stood just inside the living room. Her long dark hair was clean and shiny, and it glowed in the twinkling lights. Dark smudges marred the hollows below her shining eyes, but her cheeks were pink and healthy, her skin smooth.

She twisted her arms together, clasping her hands in front of her pale blue sweater.

"What are you doing here? I thought you weren't coming back." She sounded a little out of breath. He knew just how she felt.

He couldn't stop staring at her, drinking in the sight of her, safe and home. And his?

Maybe. If she'd have him.

He opened his mouth to answer her question, but she spoke at the same time. "Did you hear something from Amy about the charges against Juan Carlos?"

It took him a minute to get on the same track, and he stumbled over his response. "No, not really—nothing new. But she thinks it won't be long before the U.S. Attorney files the charges. They have a strong case and found more than enough evidence of international drug smuggling. And it turns out that the Panamanian authorities were looking for him, as well. He'll spend a lot of years in prison—either here or there—regretting that he ever came after you."

The tightness in her neck and shoulders relaxed. "Then why are you here?"

Will tried again to answer her, but she held up a hand to cut him off.

"I can't keep doing this. It's too hard to say goodbye every time you decide to show up and then leave again. It's not fair. Maybe it would be easier if we weren't friends."

His heart stopped beating, leaving every extremity as cold as an Alaskan winter.

Jess bit her lips together until they nearly disappeared, then hiccuped.

Heat raced through him at her giveaway. She'd been crying, and she was terrified. But he could fix this. He ran across the room, stopping just a few feet from her. She leaned back but didn't step away, so he tucked a stray piece of hair behind her ear, leaving his hand on her cheek for just a moment longer than necessary.

"Sweet Jess. I was so stupid."

She didn't argue with him, and he swallowed a chuckle.

Her bottom lip quivered. The desire to soothe it with his own nearly made him buckle, but he fought the urge. He hadn't earned the privilege of another kiss. Yet.

"Ten years ago, I left you because I was in love with you."

Her mouth fluttered briefly in a wavy smile that disappeared all too soon. "That *is* stupid."

"I know. I just thought that you belonged with Sal. I thought that was what you both wanted. I was too young to realize how jealous I was of what I thought you had. I thought if I left, my heart wouldn't be broken.

"It turned out I couldn't stop thinking about you. It didn't matter where I was, I always missed you. I'd see something and want to tell you about it, and then remember that I wasn't your best friend anymore."

She stared at her clasped hands, offering him only a glimpse of another smile. "Why the navy? You hated the thought of military school."

He couldn't keep from touching her again, so he snagged her hand, his thumb making lazy figure eights on the back of it. "The irony isn't lost on me. But it was the fastest way to get out of Dodge, and it turns out I'm not a half-bad sailor.

"Those early years, I spent most of my time trying and doing everything to forget you. But that wasn't who I wanted to be, and by the grace of God, that's not who I am now."

"Then why—" Her voice cracked, cutting off her question. She didn't try to pick up where she'd left off. She didn't need to. He knew what she was asking.

"Sal saved me from being sent to military school. All the amazing things we did during our senior year I wouldn't have been around to do if he hadn't taken the blame and the community service for me." Will fisted his hands in his pockets and squeezed his eyes shut. This was his moment of truth. "And up until an hour ago, I was sure that he was still in love with you."

"What?" Her mouth hung open in a perfect O.

Will lifted a shoulder and tugged her one step toward him. "He's my brother, and I couldn't break his heart by trying to be with you."

"But I haven't spoken to him in years."

"We didn't talk for ten, and I love you more now than I did then."

"Sal told me when we broke—" Jess's eyes grew wide, her nose wrinkling. "Did you just say…I mean, do you…do you love me?" Her last words were no more than a whisper, but he'd moved close enough that volume didn't matter.

He nodded, not even trying to fight the goofy grin he knew was plastered on his face. Digging into his pocket, he pulled out the small velvet box. Holding it in his open palm, he watched her gaze jump from his face to his hand and back again.

"Jess, can you forgive me? I wanted to stay. And now I can. Will you take me back?"

Her eyes narrowed. "What's in the box?"

"Your present. Merry Christmas."

She picked it up, her fingers pale and shaking against the black fabric. She flipped the lid back, and her teeth flashed in a giggle.

"It's just like the necklace you bought us when we were juniors." She pulled out the cheap silver charm on a fake leather strap. It was one half of a heart, with half of the inscription Best Friends.

"Almost."

Her eyebrows pinched together.

"Look at the back." He held up the other half of the charm, which dangled from a band around his wrist.

She pressed the pieces together, mouthing the words that he'd had added just for her. *And so much more.*

Closing her fist around the trinket, she leaned her forehead against his chest. She didn't wrap her arms around him, so he forced his to stay by his sides.

"Will Gumble, I've been holding on to hurts for a long time. It was easier than letting you go altogether. But I can't hold on to them anymore."

Her words were a kick to his gut, and he gasped for air, for something to keep him standing.

And then her gentle hands settled just above his belt. "I thought you didn't want to come back. I thought you were like my mom."

"I have always wanted to come back for you."

Her hands slipped around his sides and clasped at his back. "I know."

"So? Can you forgive me?"

She nestled into him, resting her ear over his heart, which felt as if it was going to pound right out of his chest. She let out a slow sigh. "I don't have room for any of that old bitterness. Not when I'm this much in love with you."

He hooked a finger under her chin and tilted

her head back to look into her eyes. "How much in love?"

She flipped her necklace over in her hand. "You did good, kid."

Leaning down, he pressed his lips to hers, warmth flooding through him. This was how it always should have been. He'd lost ten years, but he refused to lose a minute more. Pulling her closer, he ran his thumbs across her cheeks, picking up a stray tear along the way.

"So, what do you say you wear that necklace for a little while, and then I'll take you shopping for a ring? One with a diamond."

She bit her tongue but couldn't hide her spreading grin. "It's a deal."

He was smiling almost too hard to seal the deal with another kiss.

Almost.

EPILOGUE

Three months later

SEALs weren't known for picnics and parades, but when a brother on the teams had something major to celebrate, Jess had learned to count on every available man to show up.

"Will you hurry? We're going to be late," Will said, standing next to his red truck, the passenger door open wide and waiting for her.

"I'm trying." Jess scurried down the last flight of stairs from her apartment, balancing the three-tiered cake on a plate in her hands. "I know I make this look easy, but it's not."

Will chuckled as she reached his side, plucking the plate from her hands and planting a quick kiss on her lips. She leaned in just a bit, inhaling the scent of fresh rain that was uniquely him, mingled with the smell of the chocolate cake. Her hands free, she slipped them around his shoulders and deepened the connection.

"Whoa there." He pulled back, a little bit breathless, and she smiled. "This isn't the time or the place for that."

She climbed into the bucket seat and reached for the cake. "I know. But it was fun."

Will closed the door and hurried around the hood of the truck, giving it a quick smack, which made her jump, nearly dislodging the precariously balanced dessert.

She hoped her glare was palpable as he slipped behind the steering wheel and turned on the ignition. "That wasn't necessary."

"I know. But it was fun." He mimicked her tone precisely before reaching for her hand, sliding his fingers between hers and pressing the back of it to his lips.

She laughed as the butterflies that hadn't been dormant in months took flight in earnest.

"So you thought you'd make a dessert instead of buying one at the store?"

She looked down at the not-so-smoothly frosted sides of her slightly lopsided cake as he pulled onto the interstate and headed toward L.T. and Staci's home. "Sure. I thought it would be nice."

"Didn't you spend something like fifty hours in the lab this week?"

"What's that supposed to mean?"

The left corner of his mouth twitched as if he was trying to keep frowning but couldn't fight a teasing smile. "Just want to make sure one of those microscopic spores didn't manage to make it home with you and into your cake."

She playfully smacked his shoulder as his laughter pealed through the cab. "You're awful, Will Gumble. You had me really worried."

He kissed her hand again, and she leaned across the median to rest her head on his shoulder, where she left it for the rest of the silent ride.

When they pulled up in front of L.T.'s home, pink and blue balloons bounced on ribbons tied to the mailbox. Definitely Ashley's doing. Not even Staci would have announced so much to the whole neighborhood.

Matt and Ashley's SUV and Luke's coupe were already parked along the street, and Will stopped right behind his best friend's car. Then he ran around to Jess's door to help her out. She handed over her cake and hopped down, snuggling into his side as they made their way up the walk.

Before they could even ring the bell, Ashley threw the door open, greeting them with a laughing cry.

Jess hugged her friend around the two-month-old in her arms before brushing a kiss across little Nate's wispy hair.

"I'm so glad you made it." Ashley swept her free arm toward the living room. "Everyone's in there. And the food is on the island in the kitchen."

"Everyone" turned out to be Luke, Zig and Matt chatting in the corner, and Jordan talking with L.T. and Staci, who were snuggling with the newly adopted addition to their family, almost-three-year-old Winnie Grace. The little girl had visited Pacific Coast House with Staci several times over the past two months and effectively stolen the heart of everyone she met. When Winnie saw Jess, her blue eyes grew wide, and she wiggled until her dad set her on the ground. Blond ringlets bouncing, she danced around the coffee table and reached her arms up. Jess couldn't deny the sweet girl, so she plucked her up and gave her cheek a wet and wild raspberry.

Winnie squealed and flung her arms around Jess's neck. "Did you know this is my forever home? And they're my forever mommy and daddy?"

Jess suddenly couldn't swallow for the lump that filled her throat. "I did." It came out hoarse, and she tried to make up for it with a smile, all the while blinking hard against the tears in her eyes.

L.T. and Staci were going to be such amazing parents, and Jess's heart leaped just to share a fraction of their joy. Staci had always longed to be a mom, but was unable to have biological children of her own. When they'd heard about Winnie, who needed parents, they'd jumped at a chance to grow their family.

Jess couldn't help but match the smile that lit Staci's entire face.

She hadn't spent much time thinking about children of her own, but now... All she could picture were little boys with brown hair, eyes the color of milk chocolate and little dimples in their right cheeks.

Catching Will's eye across the room, she bit her bottom lip. He winked at her, but his smile faltered as his gaze turned appraising.

"Can we go outside and play on the swings with Jasper?" Winnie rescued Jess from overanalyzing what Will's look really meant.

"Sure." She corralled the youngsters through the back door and settled them in the plastic stirrups of the homemade swing set. The cousins laughed and jabbered as she took turns pushing them. After a few minutes, they hopped down and ran back inside.

Jess turned her back to the house, lifting her face to the cool breeze coming off the Pacific. Hugging herself against the chill that raced down her spine, she closed her eyes, just enjoying the moment.

Suddenly two hands slid down her arms, encircling her. She leaned against a wall of muscle and rested her head against Will's shoulder. Kissing her ear, he sighed.

"They're so happy," he said. She nodded in response. "You ever think about having kids?"

"Sometimes," she said.

His arms tightened just enough to make her smile. "What do you think about when you do?"

Her stomach rolled, another chance to choose to end the bitterness that she'd carried for sixteen years. Taking a cleansing breath, she let it go, let the reminders of her mother's betrayal vanish with the wind. "I think about how I'm never going to leave them. About how I want them to have a dad who loves them as much as my dad loves me."

She angled her head to get a look at Will's face. But she couldn't tell what he was thinking past the angle of his chin and the flex of his jaw.

"What about you?"

He shifted his weight to his other foot, his hands trembling, despite their warmth.

"Will?" She tried to pull away, but his embrace was firm.

"Mostly I think about how much I just want you to be my kids' mom."

Her pulse skittered and stopped before rushing so hard that it made everything inside her tingle.

"Jess, I love you. And I was going to wait to ask until you were sure. But I can't wait. I want to marry you so much."

His words jumbled together in her mind, and

all she could retain was one sentence. "Until I'm sure?" Forcing him to let her spin around in his arms, she hooked her hands behind his neck and tilted his head down until his gaze met hers. His chocolate eyes were swirling with uncertainty and hope.

Grabbing on to the cheap pendant at her throat, she said, "I've been sure since you gave me this."

His forehead wrinkled. "And when I deploy?"

"I have friends and family who'll be here for me." His heart galloped under her palm against his chest. "And I know you'll come back for me."

He closed his eyes, every line on his face relaxing, and he pressed his forehead to hers. "So you want to marry me or what?"

She'd have flown apart if he wasn't holding her so tight. "Definitely."

When he pressed his lips to hers, all was right with the world. She snuggled closer, ready to spend the rest of her life with this man, who had proved that he'd do anything to protect her.

"Eww!" Winnie cried from the open door. "Aunt Jess is kissing Uncle Willie!"

Will laughed against Jess's lips, his nose bumping into hers. "I think I will again, if that's okay."

"Always."

* * * * *

Dear Reader,

I'm absolutely delighted to share another book in the Men of Valor miniseries with you. I hope you enjoyed Jess and Will's story.

I first introduced Will in *A Promise to Protect,* and knew that the kid with a smart mouth was going to be a favorite of mine. Finding him just the right match in his longtime friend, Jess, was a joy.

They each carried scars from their past—Jess the bitterness of betrayal and Will the guilt of betraying her. As I wrote their story, I was reminded that forgiveness is a choice. It can feel daunting to face such deep wounds, but choosing to hang on to bitterness only gives the other person the power to cause injury again and again. When you're faced with a choice to forgive or hang on to the pain, I hope you'll choose forgiveness and trust that God is with you, giving you the strength to keep moving forward.

Thanks for spending your time with us. I'm so grateful to get to share these books with you. I'd love to hear from you. You can reach me at liz@lizjohnsonbooks.com, Twitter.com/LizJohnsonBooks, or Facebook.com/LizJohnsonBooks.

Liz Johnson

Questions for Discussion

1. Which character in this book do you most relate to? Why did you pick that person?

2. Jess and Will share a lot of history. Whose friendship have you enjoyed for the longest? Why have you stayed close?

3. Have you ever lost touch with a close friend? What do you think it would take to rekindle that friendship? Could you pick up where you'd left off ten years before?

4. Some long-distance friendships are held together by phone calls and letters, and it feels as if no time has passed when the friends are together again. Do you have any friendships like that? What makes them special?

5. Sometimes friendships end for reasons beyond just losing touch. Have you ever had a falling-out with a friend or family member? Did you reconcile with him or her? What would it take to restore your relationship?

6. Jess's mom left her when she was twelve, and it left wounds of bitterness and distrust. Have you been scarred by a past pain? How have

you dealt with it? If you were in Jess's shoes could you forgive your mom for leaving?

7. At one point Jess says that she can trust Will, but she's not sure she can forgive him. What do you think the difference between trust and forgiveness is?

8. Like Will, many of us have made bad decisions in our lives, but he tries to make up for them. What regrets have you tried to make right? What was the result of your efforts?

9. Will was prompted to change his life when he met other SEALs who were men of honor and integrity, and he realized that he needed God's help to change. Have you had a mentor or spiritual encourager who helped you make changes in your life? What was that relationship like?

10. Which scene in the book is your favorite? Why did you like it?

11. At the end of the book, Jess chooses to forgive Will, letting go of the bitterness and replacing it with love. When have you chosen to forgive someone? Did you replace that pain with something else?

12. Why do you think Will and Jess make a good match? Do you think their history will make their life together easier or harder? Why?

LARGER-PRINT BOOKS!

GET 2 FREE
LARGER-PRINT NOVELS
PLUS 2 FREE
MYSTERY GIFTS

Love Inspired®

Larger-print novels are now available...

YES! Please send me 2 FREE LARGER-PRINT Love Inspired® novels and my 2 FREE mystery gifts (gifts are worth about $10). After receiving them, if I don't wish to receive any more books, I can return the shipping statement marked "cancel." If I don't cancel, I will receive 6 brand-new novels every month and be billed just $5.24 per book in the U.S. or $5.74 per book in Canada. That's a savings of at least 23% off the cover price. It's quite a bargain! Shipping and handling is just 50¢ per book in the U.S. and 75¢ per book in Canada.* I understand that accepting the 2 free books and gifts places me under no obligation to buy anything. I can always return a shipment and cancel at any time. Even if I never buy another book, the two free books and gifts are mine to keep forever.

122/322 IDN F49Y

Name	(PLEASE PRINT)

Address	Apt. #

City	State/Prov.	Zip/Postal Code

Signature (if under 18, a parent or guardian must sign)

Mail to the Harlequin® Reader Service:
IN U.S.A.: P.O. Box 1867, Buffalo, NY 14240-1867
IN CANADA: P.O. Box 609, Fort Erie, Ontario L2A 5X3

**Are you a current subscriber to Love Inspired books
and want to receive the larger-print edition?
Call 1-800-873-8635 or visit www.ReaderService.com.**

* Terms and prices subject to change without notice. Prices do not include applicable taxes. Sales tax applicable in N.Y. Canadian residents will be charged applicable taxes. Offer not valid in Quebec. This offer is limited to one order per household. Not valid for current subscribers to Love Inspired Larger-Print books. All orders subject to credit approval. Credit or debit balances in a customer's account(s) may be offset by any other outstanding balance owed by or to the customer. Please allow 4 to 6 weeks for delivery. Offer available while quantities last.

Your Privacy—The Harlequin® Reader Service is committed to protecting your privacy. Our Privacy Policy is available online at www.ReaderService.com or upon request from the Harlequin Reader Service.

We make a portion of our mailing list available to reputable third parties that offer products we believe may interest you. If you prefer that we not exchange your name with third parties, or if you wish to clarify or modify your communication preferences, please visit us at www.ReaderService.com/consumerschoice or write to us at Harlequin Reader Service Preference Service, P.O. Box 9062, Buffalo, NY 14269. Include your complete name and address.

LILPDIR13R

Reader Service.com

Manage your account online!

- Review your order history
- Manage your payments
- Update your address

---

*We've designed
the Harlequin® Reader Service
website just for you.*

Enjoy all the features!

- Reader excerpts from any series
- Respond to mailings and special monthly offers
- Discover new series available to you
- Browse the Bonus Bucks catalog
- Share your feedback

Visit us at:
ReaderService.com